THE KNIGHT BEFORE CHRISTMAS

A KNIGHTS THROUGH TIME ROMANCE

CYNTHIA LUHRS

For everyone who loves a happy ending.

CHAPTER 1

CHARLOTTE AND HENRY

December 1337—England

Henry Thornton offered his wife a choice piece of meat only to watch as her pink cheeks turned gray and sweat dripped off her brow.

"Not again, my love?"

Charlotte clapped a hand over her mouth, the cushion falling to the floor as she pushed back from the table and fled for the garderobe.

"Shall we play a different tune, my lord?" One of the minstrels nervously watched Charlotte run through the great hall and up the stairs.

With a look to his wife's back as she rounded the corner, Henry ate the meat, knowing better than to go after her. Nay, Charlotte Merriweather Thornton would likely take his favorite blade and run him through.

Once she finished, Henry would not think upon what was happening in the garderobe—then and only then would she allow him to care for and fuss over her.

Henry chewed and swallowed the meat before answering.

"Nay. 'Tis not the music. My wife is with child." He waved a hand. "Play on."

It had cost him a good amount of coin to keep the minstrels at Ravenskirk until the new year, thus he would have them play every night until then, as it made Charlotte happy.

A servant passed by. "Have one of the lads fetch ice from the ice room and take it with cloth up to your lady."

The girl nodded, picking up the fallen cushion. "'Tis already done, my lord." She poured him more wine. "My mam says the sickness will soon pass."

"By the saints, I pray 'tis so." To see Charlotte ill and not be able to aid her... If he could take her pain as his own, Henry would see it done. A shudder ran through him. Childbirth was dangerous. He remembered Charlotte screaming. Nay, he would much prefer to face the entire French army than be a woman in childbirth.

"Where is Mama?" His son climbed up in his mother's chair, eyeing the meat knife.

"She will return soon, lad." Henry pushed the knife away from his son, but not fast enough. He snatched the apple pie from his mother's plate and ran, laughing from the hall, shoving the pie into his mouth, two of the hounds on his heels, eating the fallen bits as Henry bellowed at him to halt.

The touch of a dagger leaving his boot had Henry lifting the tablecloth, only to see the twins giggling, each one holding one of his daggers.

"Your brother is powerful fast." He held out a hand for the blades.

The twins nodded, blond curls bouncing. "Bad," they said at the same time, blue eyes narrowed at him as they shook their heads and held fast to the blades.

Henry arched a brow, as 'twas usually his daughters

making mischief and stealing pies. His son worshipped his younger twin sisters, and while Henry told his wife it did not matter if she gave birth to a boy or girl, in truth, he wished for another lad. The girls were beautiful, but their sweet faces hid the terror beneath.

A se'nnight ago, they had unraveled the scarves their Aunt Lucy made them and tied the yarn across every doorway in the castle, laughing when the servants and his guardsmen tripped. Then they had thrown all the trenchers out the windows, saying the birds were hungry.

Henry thought Charlotte was going to send them to Lucy when she found out they had taken Henry's daggers and cut off the serving girl's hair as they slept.

A shudder ran through him at the thought of what the two hellions might be plotting next as they whispered to each other, daggers clutched tightly to their chests.

"Give them to me." He frowned, but did they obey? Nay —as he reached for them, they gave a mighty tug on the tablecloth, and food, cups, and plates crashed to the floor. The wine turned the tablecloth purple and dripped on his hose.

How had Henry lost control of his household to two small females? The servants rushed to clean up the mess, throwing Henry looks that told him they knew how he was suffering.

"Saints, send me an army to fight," he mumbled. When Charlotte found out the girls had run off with his daggers... Mayhap he would seek refuge in the lists. A bit of swordplay was good for whatever ailed him. On the way outside, he stopped to praise the minstrels.

As the day faded, Henry found the twins, who refused to tell him where they had hidden his daggers, and saw them to their chamber. He had a bolt put on the outside so they could no longer sneak out during the night, though he gave them a fortnight before they figured out how to open the bolted door.

Opening the door to the chamber, Henry called out, "My love?"

"Go away and leave me alone." She moaned.

He found her sitting in a chair, wrapped in a blanket, her face the same gray as her eyes as she sipped from a cup. The scent of honey, ginger, and lemon surrounded her.

"The tea is good?"

She blinked up at him, the fire turning her hair to gold in the waning light. "It's the only thing I know I can keep down."

When he leaned down to kiss her cheek, she held her nose, pushing him away.

"Henry, I love you, but you have to move out of range of my nose. I swear, something in here smells worse than a pot of collards left on the stove for two days and two nights."

Stepping back, he discreetly sniffed himself. Nay, he did not stink.

Charlotte snorted, her hands wrapped around the warm drink. "You know everything smells to me. Our life is going to change again. I never thought we'd have four children." She patted her stomach.

Henry hoped in time they would have one or two more, for he loved children and being a father. 'Twas his greatest joy, after his wife.

"You look beautiful… but tired." He sat on the rug at her feet and slipped her shoe off, taking her foot in his hands, rubbing and kneading until she groaned in pleasure. "Better?"

She wriggled the other foot at him. "It will be soon."

With a grin, he ran his hand up her calf.

CHAPTER 2

THE THEFT AND LORD GORGES

WHEN THEY HAD COME to the castle, Oliver and the other minstrels gaped as they looked about. The castle was built in a square with four round towers, surrounded by water on all sides, with chunks of ice floating in the water. Oliver could not swim, and crossed himself as they passed over the bridge, praying he would not fall in and drown.

Inside the great hall, the walls were whitewashed, some painted with scenes of animals, flowers, and ferocious battle scenes. There were tapestries on the walls featuring bees, butterflies, flowers, and animals. Patterned tiles covered the floors. There were white tablecloths on the trestle tables, with ceramic wine jugs and ale flagons up and down all the tables.

The table where the lord and lady sat had cushions on the benches, a silver salt cellar, and enameled silver drinking cups. Oliver looked around Ravenskirk Castle as he and the other minstrels finished eating. Lord Ravenskirk was a wealthy man.

While Oliver was singing during supper, he had watched the lady of the household. She was exquisite with her gray eyes and long blond hair she wore in a braid. But it was the necklace that captured his attention. Lady Ravenskirk touched it many times, the charms bright in the torchlight.

During their travels, Oliver had heard tales of a powerful necklace, but he had heard the bandit of the wood owned the necklace. 'Twas rumored to be bewitched by a powerful fairy and would aid whoever owned it. The lord and lady had more than enough. Oliver had a desperate need of a magic necklace.

That night, when the household was quiet, the dogs asleep in front of the hearths, curled up with the servants, he rose from his pallet on the floor of the great hall, not knowing how but that he must have the necklace. As he crept through the hall, a glint caught his eye.

A servant mumbled in his sleep and turned over, causing Oliver to pause. He held his breath, waiting until he was certain the man would not wake. Making not a sound, he knelt by the cushions at the lord's table. It was caught on the cloth and came free when he picked up the cushion. 'Twas the necklace. For a moment, he held it in his fist, watching the charms turn and catch the faint light from the fire.

Helena. The thought of her filled his heart. When Lady Ravenskirk fled the hall, she must have dropped it, and neither her children nor her husband had found it. 'Twas as if they had not seen it—'twas a sign from the fates, meant for him.

He looked around the hall. Assured no one was awake and watching him, Oliver closed his hand over the necklace, noticing the broken chain. No one had come looking for it, but they would soon notice such a powerful charm had gone missing.

Before he could change his mind, Oliver crept back to his pallet and tucked the necklace into the small satchel containing his meager belongings. Once his heart calmed, he closed his eyes, one arm around the satchel, and fell into a restless sleep.

'Twas with a start that Oliver woke early, knowing he must not stay and be found out, for he was now a thief. Unless... he could go to Lord Ravenskirk and tell him he found the necklace. The lord would give him gold for returning such a valuable piece. But nay, he had more need than the lord and lady.

Lord Gorges would accept the charmed necklace in trade for Helena. His betrothed.

Two years had passed since he saw her at the market. With one smile, Oliver knew they belonged together. He went to her father, asked for her hand in marriage, but alas, the man would not agree. Helena's sire said his eldest daughter needs stay home and take care of her sisters and household.

Those in the village had told Oliver over a cup of ale that the father was a drunk. The man had fallen off a roof, breaking both legs, and could no longer labor for his family. Helena's mother had died of a sickness many years ago, so 'twas left to Helena to take care of them all. The man beat his daughters. Helena begged him to let her come with them, but Oliver had not wanted to steal her away, he wanted to marry her in front of a priest in the chapel, so he told her to wait and he would come for her.

When he came back for her, she was gone. A fortnight later, Oliver had seen his beloved. He and the other minstrels had played at a great house and were on their way to the next home when he saw her in the local market.

Filled with joy, he ran to her, only to find out her father had sold her to Lord Gorges.

All knew Lord Gorges did not care for minstrels or merrymaking of any kind. Oliver begged her forgiveness for not stealing her away. He promised to make her his. Helena kissed and blessed him, swore she would wait for him, no matter how long it would take.

The villagers knew Lord Gorges. The man would never let a servant go, so Oliver would use the magic of the necklace to trade for his love.

CHAPTER 3

LUCY AND WILLIAM

L

ucy Merriweather Brandon, now Lady Blackford, wound a small ball of yellow yarn and stuffed it in the pocket of her dress as she made her way through the great hall and outside. The crisp air filled her lungs, and Lucy swore she'd never thought she'd enjoy winter and snow as much as she had since traveling through time.

After days of whirling snow and molten silver skies, the sun had finally come out. Not the scorching, turn-your-insides-to-liquid sun, and certainly not the make-you-feel-like-you-were-in-a-shower humidity, Holden Beach summer day, but no matter—she'd take any bit of sun she could get.

She turned her face to the sky, listening to the servants coming and going, the clang of the blacksmith at work, and the sound of men practicing with swords and daggers in the lists. Were her ancestors turning over in their graves that she and her sisters had broken with tradition and officially used their husband's last names? Though many folks still knew they were the Merriweather Sisters.

"Oof, sorry, lady." One of William's knights bumped into

her when she stopped suddenly, the epiphany hitting her like a lightning bolt.

"'Tis my fault. Woolgathering."

He nodded and went on his way as she moved out of the way and sat down on a stone bench leaning against the wall. The heavy black woolen cloak over her dress, along with her crocheted scarf and mittens, kept her warm. Thinking about family traditions, she pulled the hood tighter around her face to keep the wind out and the scarf up over her nose, the scent of wool and the herbs used for the dye, reminding her of spring.

Had she and her sisters been the ones responsible for starting the tradition that all Merriweather women kept their maiden names? Could they have done it so that, hundreds of years later, they would be able to find each other when they traveled through time? And thereby ensuring the tradition was passed on, had made it come true? It was the simplest explanation and made complete sense.

"Lucy. My love?"

The shadow blocking out the sun startled her.

"William. I didn't hear you."

Her husband chuckled, with just a touch of gravel, as he leaned down, pulled the deep yellow scarf down, and kissed her soundly, heating the blood in her veins to near boiling.

"'Tis obvious. I have been calling your name, and here you sit, lost in thought. Is aught amiss?"

He sat beside her, steam rolling off him from his exertions in the lists. The warmth from his body made her snuggle closer.

"No. I was just thinking about tradition." Lucy tucked a silver and brown lock behind her ear. She kept it loose and down in the cold months to help keep her neck warm.

After all these years, those green eyes and crooked nose

still made her shiver. William was six foot four to her five foot six, and they fit together perfectly.

Sure, they were older now, but as far as she was concerned, they were in the prime of their lives, and at the age of fifty-three, Lucy found she no longer cared what people thought.

With each passing year, she found it easier to say no to things she didn't want to do without feeling the least bit guilty.

William was fifty-five, yet still had defined muscles and a full head of thick, glossy brown hair. She remembered how Aunt Pittypat used to complain about men her friends dated that were losing their hair in their forties. Maybe the everyday physical labor and swordplay kept him young?

"My lady wife." William pulled her closer. The scent of leather, steel, and wool filled her nose as he held her. "You are far away today. Tell me your thoughts."

"You know how my sisters and I keep our name Merriweather?"

"Aye. I have taken much jesting over your choice." He stretched booted feet out in front of him, brushing dust off his black tunic and hose.

Lucy turned to face him. "What if my sisters and I started the tradition and made sure those who came after us kept their names so that, hundreds and hundreds of years from now, my sisters and I would be able to find each other?"

She watched him ponder the thought.

"From the tales you have told me, I would believe such. The Merriweather women are a fearsome bunch."

The corner of his mouth turned up. "I have something which may please you." William handed her a letter, creased and tattered along the edges, having passed through many hands to reach Blackford. "From your sister, Charlotte."

"How? In such weather?" Lucy squealed, pulling off her mittens and snatching the letter from his hands.

"The men believe her to be touched by the fae. She is able to send letters through all weather and skirmishes."

"I would think the messengers would get the credit for delivering the letters, not my sister." Lucy broke the seal and opened the letter. Seeing her sister's familiar handwriting had her wiping her eyes.

"Mayhap the messengers are swift of foot and horse because they believe your sister to be charmed." William chuckled. "If she were leading these skirmishes for our sire, they would be over before they began."

He stretched his arms over his head, cracking his knuckles. "This war you tell of that will last a hundred years would be over in a fortnight with your sister in charge."

Lucy heard bits and pieces of what William was saying, but she was too engrossed in her sister's news.

"She is rather bossy," he said, and elbowed her. "Charlotte scares me. Henry must sleep with one eye open."

"I'm sure he sleeps fine, as long as he's on her good side."

She cut her eyes at him, and William held up his hands. "Aye, I will be quiet until you finish reading." He couldn't resist adding, "But don't tell her I said thus; she would never let me forget it."

Leaning over, Lucy kissed him. "Your secret is safe with me."

When she read the second page, Lucy gasped. "Shut the front door!" Leave it to Charlotte to save the big news for last. "Did you read this?"

William shook his head. "The seal was unbroken. I do not read letters from your sister. What news?"

"Melinda told Charlotte that she now knows the 'real story' about Aunt Pittypat and Aunt Mildred, one that

Melinda says will make us feel different about cranky Aunt Mildred, and she says we have a niece."

Their breath puffed out in front of them as they talked, yet curled up next to William, she was warm enough to stay outside a bit longer. This time of year, it was darker than usual in the castle, and Lucy found herself going outdoors whenever she could.

"Are you sad you will never know her?" he asked gently as he wrapped a lock of her hair around his finger.

"That's the thing. Her name is Chloe, and she…" Lucy looked around before lowering her voice and leaning close to his ear. "She traveled through time too. Chloe was living with Mildred, and now she's here. I'm dying to know the details, which, of course, she's left out."

"Come inside before you freeze. Melinda will send another letter." William stood, pulling her to her feet.

"Not yet. Let's stay outside a bit longer." She shook her head. "She'll be planning another letter with more teasers so we'll beg her to tell us or make a trip to visit."

"Spring would be better," he said.

Lucy clapped her hands together. "You have a messenger leaving tomorrow?"

He nodded as he walked her to the lists.

"Perfect. I'll send gifts and bribe her to tell us. She can't resist my ginger candy."

William kissed her cheek. "No one can resist your candy, love." Then he let go of her, unsheathed his sword, and bellowed at the men, "Come on, by twos now."

Grinning, Lucy left him to his swordplay. She'd send a letter to Charlotte as well, telling her the plan to bribe their sister and find out the big news. No way was she waiting until spring.

The delay in news arriving was something Lucy had

gotten used to over the years, but now and then she lamented the loss of the internet and the instantaneous communication afforded by texting. A laugh escaped as she pictured William and his knights with swords slung up on their shoulders, pausing to send texts.

CHAPTER 4

CHRISTIAN AND ASHLEY

Ashley pulled her hair into a bun, pursing her lips as she examined the ends. It was halfway down her back and desperately needed the split ends trimmed. She was almost finished tying a green ribbon around her bun to match her dress when she heard the commotion in the corridor.

"Where is my wife?" Christian Thornton, Lord Winterforth, pushed the door open to their chamber and leaned over, hands on his knees, gasping for breath.

"What's wrong?" She grabbed the fur-lined cloak from a peg on the wall and went to him. His face was red, and he was sweating.

He held out a hand. "We were cutting the greenery you wanted to decorate the hall when he said he could not marry her."

Ashley grabbed her husband by the arm and dragged him out of the corridor as he gasped like a fish on a dock. "Oh yes he will. It's just cold feet."

"He is… wearing his boots, love. 'Tis… cold outside." Christian gasped as she pulled him down the stairs and through the great hall, where she paused to direct several servants.

She pointed to the hearth closest to them. "The greenery also goes around the doorways. Did you finish decorating the tree outside?"

"Aye, lady."

She nodded and walked outside, looking to the clear skies. Thank goodness it was going to be a beautiful day for a wedding—if they could get the groom to put on his big-boy pants. She pulled her husband toward the garrison. "Where is he?"

"The stables." Christian turned her in the opposite direction.

She narrowed her eyes at him. Merrick and Arthur had sworn they were not the ones sneaking the treats she'd been making in preparation for Christmas. Her adopted sons had tried to blame their sister, Mary, who'd sniffed and said "whatever," making Christian laugh and Ashley cringe. She tried so hard not to use too many words from her own time, but occasionally they slipped out.

"Have you been sneaking sweets again? Why are you so out of breath?"

"Ulrich stole my horse, I ran all the way back from the hunt, the bloody whoreson," her husband snarled.

At five foot seven, she was only a head shorter than Christian. Now and then, Ashley wished for super-high plat-form heels so she could look down her nose at him when he made her mad. Which wasn't often, but when he did, Ashley could hardly see straight.

For a moment she stared at her husband, appreciating his form and looks as one would a beautiful painting. He and his brothers looked like movie stars with their golden hair and chiseled jaws.

Blue eyes gazed back at her. "Your eyes turn dark green and the freckles above your brow turn dark brown when you're angry, my love."

She arched a brow. "Then Ulrich best beware."

They entered the stables, following the smell of alcohol to one of the empty stalls. Ashley lifted her dress as she stepped over a bundle, and then blinked as it moved.

Christian swore and nudged the bundle with his shoe. He had forgone his normal tunic, hose, and boots for the latest fashion. The fitted jacket was so tight that she hoped he wouldn't have to swing a sword, and the sleeves were huge and would drag through the gravy at the wedding feast, but wisely, she didn't say a word. It was true what a friend of hers back home had said about married couples looking and dressing alike. They were both dressed in green velvet and silk, though he would always have better hair. Why did men get the full, dark eyelashes and fabulous hair? Something she'd ponder after she kicked the groom in the butt and got him moving.

Everything was planned. The minstrels would play at the feast, and the goose and mince pies were cooking along with the rest of the food. The kitchens would be working over-time to feed everyone they'd invited, as they'd decided to combine the Yule celebration with the wedding.

"Leave me be," Ulrich mumbled, sending a noxious cloud of alcoholic fumes through the air.

"You have got to be kidding me. How much has he had to drink?" Ashley breathed shallowly through her mouth. "He'll set the stables on fire."

"Do not ask—" Christian started.

"A great deal, lady. Might ye have more?" Ulrich slurred.

Oh, this wasn't good. "Gwen will be furious," Ashley said. "She might take a blade to you herself and save me the trouble." She scowled at her husband and his guardsman. "Hrumph." She rolled her eyes. Men. Sometimes they drove her crazy.

"I'm going to find Gwen and stall for time. Get Ulrich sobered up." She pinched her nose. "And dump a bucket of water over him. He stinks."

As she turned to leave, Ashley called out, "Get him to the chapel or you'll be sleeping with your precious sheep." Her husband had a thriving wool trade, part of it legal, the rest part of a smuggling operation.

Now to find the priest. She ran out of the stables, wishing the entire time for a huge mug of strong black coffee. Ashley rounded the building, muttering under her breath.

If Christian didn't get Ulrich on his feet, her husband's guardsman would be sorry when Ashley finished with him. He'd be out on the battlements until spring.

A dunk in the river would sober him up, though she better let Christian handle it. As annoyed as she was, she'd push Ulrich off the bridge and hope for the best. Could he swim? Ashley shook her head, mentally making a note to have a few men on hand who could swim, just in case her temper got the best of her.

CHRISTIAN COULDN'T WAIT to give Ashley his Yule gift after the feast. At great expense, he had purchased books for her. Enough for her to read for a year. She had been jesting with him for months about his gift. But one of the stable boys had been so excited that he told Christian that Ashley had purchased the horse he'd wanted and hidden the animal in a stable at the inn in the village.

Ulrich swayed back and forth, his hair wet and tied back, his clothes clean as Christian gaped.

"What did you do to him?" He glared at Morien.

The smuggler grinned, showing a go`ld tooth. "Yer wife thought a swim in the river would do the man a bit of good." He stroked his black beard. "I am always happy to oblige a lady."

Christian had to admit that Ulrich looked and smelled much better. He still wobbled a bit when he walked, but he would do.

"And the other?"

The smuggler said, "The lads left the goods and took the wool, as discussed. No one will notice them on the river this night. 'Tis too cold. I will stay for the wedding and the feast." Morien let out a gusty sigh. "I do love a wedding."

This was news to Christian. "I did not know you had a wife."

"Oh aye, I have had four wives." The man counted them off on his fingers, each adorned with a gold ring. He had dark eyes and black hair that made men cross themselves when they came across the smuggler.

"Are you still aiding those in need? I heard tell of doings that must have been you."

Christian smiled. "I do what I can when I can." He nodded to Ulrich. "Ashley and I will see Ulrich and Gwen settled in a home of their own. I could use a lookout on the other side of the river."

One of the servants stopped in front of them. "My lady says 'tis time."

Morien clapped Christian on the back. "I've men posted outside the chapel in case he makes a run for it." Then the smuggler laughed. "If he does not marry her, I will. 'Tis time I took wife number five."

Unsure if the smuggler was jesting, Christian told him, "Ulrich loves the girl. The men were telling him once married, his wife would only please him until she had a babe."

The smuggler arched a brow. "Not the wives I've had."

"We are entering the chapel, man. Not now." Then Christian grinned. "Tell me after."

CHAPTER 5

THOMAS WILTON

HE MISSED her more in winter. When the land was sleeping, the silence of the realm broken only by the sound of his horse. The silver sky reminded Thomas Wilton of her hair, and he swore Penelope's laughter echoed on the wind as it blew through the forest, tormenting him with her loss.

Duty and responsibility. Family. They had been all that mattered to him. In the end, when he got what he wanted, when she sent him back to his own time, Thomas knew. Love was truly all that mattered in this life. Penelope had sacrificed their love so he could have what he told her he wanted. Truly, he was a dolt.

The horse snorted as Thomas patted the beast.

"Aye, Holden. 'Tis going to be a cold day."

He rode out of the wood into a clearing, where a small inn leaned to one side. Light from the windows spilled out, turning the snow to gold.

A sleepy lad met him in the courtyard. "See to my horse." He handed the great black beast's reins to the boy.

"Aye, sir." The lad pocketed the coin Thomas tossed to him with a grin when the silver appeared.

When Thomas opened the door to the inn, he blinked against the light, the noise, and the warmth as it seeped into his bones. He felt the cold steel of the daggers in his boots as he followed a serving wench to a table and bench near the fire.

The wall against his back, Thomas kept his cloak about him and stretched his booted feet out in front of him.

"A right cold night tonight." The wench set a platter bearing ale, bread, and a hearty stew that made his stomach rumble on the table in front of him.

"Aye, it is." He rubbed a hand through his hair, almost too weary to lift the spoon. "I thank ye."

With each year that passed since she had sent him back, Thomas grew more melancholy and restless. When the end of the year drew nigh, he'd take to wandering the realm, unable to find comfort with his kin and their well-meaning smiles.

After spending a fortnight with his family this year, Thomas had ridden away from Oakwick Manor without looking back.

In the years since the fire, Heath had added on to Oakwick. Thomas' half-brother had grown into a fine man, a wealthy wool merchant, with babes of his own. Three fine lads.

For the past fortnight, Thomas had felt his age, old wounds paining him, letting him know the weather would turn from the ache in his bones.

His half-sister, Josephine, had asked him to stay until spring and then travel with her to her estate. She too had made an advantageous marriage. With two girls and two boys, she had been blessed.

Penelope would be filled with joy to know her sacrifice had not been in vain. Thomas had been returned to his time, during August in the Year of Our Lord 1305. And at the exact moment the ground had opened up, but this time, Roger and the two remaining attackers were the ones who were taken by the storm. Roger DeChartes would never wed Josephine, never be master of Oakwick. 'Twas everything Thomas had wanted, but was not enough. He would trade all that he owned, even his soul, for one more night with her.

When Thomas came to and found himself looking over the edge of the cliff, seeing his attackers fall instead of him, he fell to his knees screaming to the heavens, beseeching the fates to send him back to his beloved, but 'twas not to be. In the ensuing years, he saw his bastard siblings were well provided for, never having to worry. Yet Thomas was restless, unable to stay at Oakwick or to share in their happiness.

Everywhere he went, he saw her face. Wondered what she was doing in her own time. Or would be doing when she was born hundreds of years from now. Would she wed another? Did she think of him still?

Deep in his heart, Thomas knew Penelope had sacrificed their love so he could go home. Right the wrongs done to his family. But in the darkness of night, when the wind blew through the trees, the snow turning the land white and silver, he turned angry with her, wished he could bellow and stomp about, scowling at her. But alas, she was not yet born, and he would never see her again. His beloved. His wife.

The wooden bench creaked as he shifted, the noise of the tavern sounding far away. There was an ocean of time separating them. Might he still find his way back one day?

Whenever there was a storm, Thomas would prick his finger with the dagger she had given him and beseech the fates, but no matter how many times, how many years passed, he had never been able to travel to the future again.

He touched his sword, stroking the hilt. The blade he had thought lost and then found again in the sea at Holden Beach.

"Penelope," he murmured as he stared into the crackling fire, the warmth lulling him to sleep.

"Anything else?" The serving woman leaned down, displaying her ample bosom.

With a yawn, he stretched. "A room for the night." Then, seeing her grin, he amended, "My lady wife awaits my return."

The woman sniffed. "Come along with ye."

He would spend another day at the inn before traveling onward. To where he did not know, nor did he care.

Thomas followed her to a small room, already warm from the fire crackling in the hearth.

"I'll bring ye more ale."

He nodded and sat down on the small bed, pulling off his boots, eager for sleep. For when he slept, he would dream. The dreams so real he felt the heat of the sun, heard the gulls, the crash of the waves, and once again saw her face. Felt her in his arms, the scent of her on his skin after he had loved her well through the night.

Would he ever find a place to call home? Might he one day find peace?

CHAPTER 6

ALBIN AND CLARA AT BLACKFORD CASTLE

WHEN WAS he going to kiss her? Clara frowned, hands on her hips, listening to Albin go on and on about his swordplay. He had arrived at Blackford when he was eight, a se'nnight before Lord Blackford had been granted the castle for saving his king. Clara arrived a year later, all of eight years old.

She'd taken one look at Albin and known he was the boy she wanted to plight her troth. Her mam, rest her soul, had said the same about Clara's da. They had passed years ago, but her ma said she knew the day she saw him; he was the only man for her. Her mam had been ten when she first saw the boy who would grow up to be Clara's da.

Albin had risen to second-in-command under Thomas in Lady Blackford's personal guard. Now he was almost two score, Clara had waited for him all her life, and at thirty-seven years, she was still a maiden. The other women in the kitchens teased her, saying Albin was married to his sword and would never take her to wife, but Clara knew 'twas fated they would be together.

Why had he waited so long? He held a secure position in the guard, had a roof over his head, food, and a bed. What sign did he seek? She scowled and adjusted the basket on her hip.

Albin rocked back on his heels, stroking his chin, as his captain did when thinking. Biting her cheek so she would not laugh, Clara wanted to tell Albin he was just as fierce. Her heart ached for the boy filled with laughter. The man before her was much too serious.

"Thomas says Lord Blackford is sending men to fight, and we must double the guard on the secret passages." Albin shuffled his feet, the blue tunic and hose making his dark hair seem black as night.

She held in the fear, pushed it deep within herself. "You are important to our lady. Surely you would not go?"

"Nay, I am needed here." He sounded sad. Men could be such dolts.

"I would not wish harm to come to you." The wind blew, and she pulled the hood on her cloak close, grateful for the scarf her lady had given her.

"If a war is coming, mayhap 'tis time to take—"

"Clara. Clara, where are you?" Louisa called from the kitchens.

"Coming," Clara yelled back, shifting the basket of greens she had picked from the greenhouse. It was warm in there, and she loved spending time with all the growing things and the fresh scent of dirt.

With a last longing look at Albin, she sighed. Men. They needed a firm hand. A woman to tell them their own mind. Clara was tired of waiting for Albin to decide he loved her. Tired of the other women calling her old maid.

Nay, she would make sure Albin took her to wed before the year ended, even if she had to twist his ear and drag him to the chapel herself.

Not looking where she was stomping, she hit a wall and bounced backward, the basket falling. Before she could cry out, Lord Blackford caught her in one arm and the basket in the other.

"Easy, lass."

"I'm sorry, my lord." She cringed. Lord Blackford was so fearsome that at times he frightened her.

"William. Stop scowling; you'll scare her." Lady Blackford smiled. "Clara, are you hurt? My husband does not look when he stomps about."

"No, lady. I am unharmed." Clara smoothed her dress. Her lady was beautiful and kind, and everyone at Blackford loved her.

"Go on, William. I'll catch up." Lady Blackford kissed her husband, making Clara sigh.

"What's wrong?" Lady Blackford walked beside Clara as Louisa called out again.

Clara turned to her mistress and snorted. "'Tis Albin. I have been waiting for him to propose since I was eight. And I am still waiting almost a score and ten years later." She scowled at the men in the lists. "I am tired of waiting. I know there is no other. Why does he not take me to wife?"

Her lady leaned close, blue eyes full of laughter. "I find men rarely know their own minds. You must lead them where you want them to go." She looked around. "And sometimes, you must give them a push."

"Aye, lady. He will marry me before the year is done. I want a husband, and none other will do."

"I have no doubt with your guidance he will come to his senses." Lady Blackford clapped her hands. "We will have a Yule wedding."

They crossed the muddy courtyard, making their way to the kitchens, Lady Blackford talking about the wedding as if it would happen. Her excitement filled Clara, who decided yes, she would wed Albin before the year ended. Now to plot and get him to propose.

CHAPTER 7

LORD GORGES

THE SMALL CASTLE had been in disrepair for years before Peter, Lord Gorges, inherited it from his father, along with a handful of servants, all as pinched and sullen as he and his father, and his father before him. One servant had died and the other two followed soon after, leaving him with a cook and a stable boy—until he found Helena.

A lowly servant who cleaned and emptied his chamber pot. Like his father, he saw no need for a modern garderobe, nor did he want the expense of adding on to his home.

The girl smelled of apples. Peter did not know why he had agreed to buy her from the drunk, but 'twas a small amount of coin, and there was something in her smile that made him pause.

The villagers said Peter was like his father, tight-fisted and solitary, bent over, with a grating voice and red-rimmed eyes.

Peter sat hunched over on his stool, a blanket about his shoulders, close to the fire. The girl brought him watered-down wine, not spiced or warm, for why should he have the expense? Peter did not care if 'twas cold, nor did he care what others said about him, for his temperament was as frosty as the weather.

"Shall I build up the fire for ye, my lord?" The girl shivered in the gloom, rubbing her arms.

He eyed her sharply. "Nay, I want no roaring fire so you and the servants may bask by the fire when I am abed. I will not waste my coin."

She did not falter. "Shall I have the stable boy cut greenery for Yule?"

"Yule. Hrumph."

At this, Helena pursed her lips. "Will you take supper in the hall?"

He growled at her. "I will eat in my solar. See that the cook does not waste any meat."

Finished with his supper, Peter heard the girl singing softly as she took his trencher away.

"Why do you sing? Are you so full of joy?"

She helped him to the stool in front of the meager fire. "My betrothed always had a tune ready. Singing keeps me close to him."

"Hrumph. Singing is a terrible waste of breath. You have no betrothed. You belong to me, as do the candlesticks, the stool, and my blankets."

There was a knock at the door, so with his leave, she went to see who it might be. No one visited him. No one visited his father.

When she returned, it was with three children dressed in rags.

"My lord, if it pleases ye, these little ones are hungry and seek a bed for the night. Might they sleep in the stables and have the trencher from supper to share amongst them?" She rubbed her hands together, waiting for his answer.

Peter sneered. "Why should I give of what is mine to feed them? Let them labor for their food and bed."

"They have nowhere to go, and it is a cold night. If we do not aid them, they will most likely die."

Uncaring of the orphans staring at him, Peter said, "Good. There are too many of those who wish to be given what belongs to others. Let them die. I only wish to be left alone." He turned away from them on the stool. "Go away and leave me be."

As he was nodding off, Helena returned, standing before him.

"Speak, girl. What do you want?"

"'Tis Yule soon. Might I visit my betrothed—I mean, my family? I would only be gone a se'nnight."

"A se'nnight? And who will labor in your stead?" Lord Gorges demanded.

Her eyes leaked as she sniffled.

"Do not weep. I despise womanly weeping."

"My lord, I beseech ye. I will not ask again, only this one time."

He let out a heavy sigh. "Go then, but do not tarry, or I will see you whipped."

"Thank ye, my lord." She scurried from the solar, leaving him alone. When the fire went out, 'twas dark, but Peter liked the darkness. Darkness meant he was not spending his gold.

The door to his chamber shut and bolted, Peter looked into the small fire in the hearth and gasped. The embers showed him his father's face. Then he blinked, and the apparition was gone.

"Hrumph."

Stiff, he sat staring at the embers, willing his body to move to the bed. The bells from the abbey rang, waking him. They sounded as if in his very chamber.

Then came a noise like the long-disused portcullis being

raised. No one came through the gates, and with no guards-men, it remained raised.

The bells were so loud that he could not hear, and he slapped hands to his ears to shut out the noise.

"Make it stop," he pleaded.

The door to his chamber opened with a bang, as if a gust of wind blew it open—but how was that possible when he himself had bolted the door?

There in the gloom was a spirit. His father's image gazed back at him.

"How... What..." Peter crossed himself.

The spirit looked about the chamber. "'Tis the same as when 'twas mine." The spirit took a step closer. "I am in purgatory. I did not learn in life to cast off my chains. You, my son, will meet the same fate if you do not change."

The apparition before him was faded; the bare stone wall could be seen through his father's image. But 'twas his father's image and chilled him to his very soul.

Then the current Lord Gorges narrowed his eyes. Doubt filled him. "You are merely an apparition from spoilt meat in the stew, or the wine had turned. My sire is long dead."

The spirit moved closer. "When you had but ten winters, you hid in the chest at the foot of the bed in your mother's chamber. I found you asleep in your own shite."

Terror filled Peter's veins. No one knew this but his father. "Why do you torment me? We are the same."

"We are. So you too will be bound in chains for all eterni-ty." The chains wrapped around his father from head to toe clinked on the stone as the spirit took another step closer.

"Would you give me comfort this night? Take away my fear, Father?"

His father shook his head, the chains about his neck rattling with the movement. "I have no comfort to give, and you deserve none. I am unable to linger in one place, nor to rest. Cursed by the fates to wander for all time."

"Why are you tormented, sire? You left behind much gold."

"Bah, what is gold against a soul?" The spirit moaned. "This time of the year, I suffer the most. So many regrets."

The spirit looked to the window. "I needs take my leave." He pointed a bony finger at Peter. "You have a chance to escape my fate."

The spirit started to fade. "Three spirits will visit you this night. Each one will show you the meaning of Yule. Embrace joy, my son, or you too will be cursed by the fates for all eternity."

He took one step into the dying fire. "The first spirit comes on the morrow."

Then the spirit walked into the fire and vanished.

Peter rubbed his eyes. He leapt forward, stirring the embers, his hand shaking, his breath shallow, but his father was gone.

CHAPTER 8

EDWARD AND JENNIFER

LADY SOMERFORTH STOOD BACK, tapping the end of the paint-brush against her chin as she studied the work in progress. Edward had surprised her by giving her one of the storage rooms for her very own studio. It hadn't taken long for her to break in the room.

At first he couldn't understand why she didn't want tapestries on the walls or rugs on the floors. After about a month, he understood and thanked her for saving him the expense. To which she'd replied that she had probably cost him more than the tapestries and rugs, considering all the supplies she'd purchased. Thank goodness he just laughed and told her to buy whatever she needed. He knew she wouldn't go crazy.

Her husband and his brothers might be wealthy, but hard times were coming, and she'd never been one to overspend.

Everywhere she looked was a riot of color, though it wasn't purposeful. More like something Jackson Pollock would wholeheartedly approve of as he walked around the room with a cigarette dangling from the corner of his mouth.

There was paint on the walls, spattered across the floor,

and a slash of blue across the wooden door, like one of the guys in the movie *Braveheart* had slid down the door, or maybe a bunch of blueberries had met an untimely demise.

A snort escaped. Maybe she should open the window, even if it was cold. She was getting silly inhaling the turpentine and paint, but she loved the smell.

Until she'd traveled through time, she'd never noticed that stone had a smell. When the walls were damp, she noticed it more; it was a pleasant smell, and mixed with the scents of her studio—well, she'd just say it was an interesting perfume, and she was glad Edward liked the way she smelled.

Cold air filled the room and cleared her head as Jennifer threw open the shutters. It was a beautiful day. From here, she could see the now dormant gardens as she leaned against the wall. In the spring, the scent from the roses would be overwhelming, the colors providing her endless inspiration.

"What are you humming?"

With a shriek, she dropped the brush, yellow paint splattering across the stone floor to mix with the other colors, so many that they nearly obscured the color of the stone.

"Edward. You scared me."

Edward Thornton, Lord Somerforth, gathered her in his arms and kissed her soundly. He squinted as he looked at her and chuckled.

"You have a smudge of red on your cheek." He wiped it off and kissed her again. "And a bit of green on your chin." He kissed her again. "Right there."

When he pulled back, she saw a tiny spot of green on his lip and smiled.

"What was the tune you were humming, wife?"

"'Wild Is the Wind' by Nina Simone." She took the messy bun down and rewound her long black hair so it was up and out of the way while she painted. He loved her long hair, but she'd learned the hard way to put it up, or she'd end up with paint in her hair. And no way was she cutting it off again.

"There are some days I miss not being able to turn on my favorite satellite radio stations or go see the latest movie. I wonder what's popular now?"

"The satellite is the machine in the sky?" His tunic had a rip in the sleeve, but upon looking closer, she didn't see any blood. He was dusty and sweaty and had never looked better.

"Yep. They can tell if you brushed your hair today or if your horse has a spot of white on his head."

"They can see so far?" He looked out the window as if he could see the satellite all the way in the future. "And they do not fall from the sky?"

She shook her head. "It's rare. When I left, there was talk about small machines called drones that could be used to deliver things you bought."

"Such wondrous marvels." Edward said softly, "Do you regret your choice? Or ever wish you had gone back? To your home?" He stood still as a tree, waiting.

Jennifer wrapped her arms around him, inhaling his scent. "I don't have any regrets, and no, I don't wish I'd gone back, because then I wouldn't have you. The stuff I tell you about is just stuff. Things. *You* are my home."

She looked up at her husband, her heart beating faster. He looked like a movie star with his naturally highlighted blond hair and green eyes. The man was a good six foot four and muscled from swinging a sword about. He'd recently turned forty to her thirty.

Jennifer had recently wondered if she was having a bit of a midlife crisis—not that she'd ever let on. There was something about turning thirty that was bothering her. Nothing she could put a finger on yet. Before she could think about why, there was a wail and their son came toddling in, clutching a wriggling puppy to his chest.

"My doggy," he said, stroking the hound's silky ears.

Alice skidded to a stop. "My lord. My lady. This little lad has been very naughty today."

Wilson was two. They'd given him Jennifer's maiden name. He crawled and walked early, terrorizing the young woman who helped look after him.

"What has he done this time?" Edward crossed his arms over his chest, his feet shoulder width apart and a frown on his face.

"He put a frog in my bed, the wee imp." Alice held out her hands for the puppy, but Wilson darted away, chanting, "Mine, mine, mine."

Before Jennifer could say a word, Edward had picked up their son and scowled at him. "What did I tell ye, lad?"

Wilson scrunched up his face. "Don't 'member."

Edward handed the squirming puppy over to Alice and stared down at their son, making Jennifer clap a hand over her mouth so she wouldn't laugh at the identical frowns on their faces. Her husband's lip twitched, but he held his ground.

"We mind mistress Alice."

"Nay." The boy shook his head, black curls bobbing. He'd inherited her hair and Edward's eyes. Green eyes narrowed at green eyes, and Jennifer knew he was going to be a stubborn handful as he grew up, like someone else she knew and loved.

Edward held Wilson by his tunic and growled. "To the lists, then."

Their son squealed with delight as Edward tossed him in the air and caught him.

"More, Da. More," he demanded.

With a kiss on her cheek, her husband held up Wilson, so she could ruffle his hair. "Be good for Daddy."

Wilson clapped his chubby hands together. "Swords." He chortled.

"That's my lad," Edward said, striding toward the door.

"Like father, like son," Jennifer called out. Facing the painting, the world faded away as she picked up her brush, wiped it off, and decided yes, a bit more blue in the stonework.

CHAPTER 9

JOHN AND ANNA

JOHN THORNTON, Lord Blackmoor, stood in the newly opened chamber on the fourth floor of Blackmoor Castle and slowly turned in a circle. Surrounded by bogs and moors, he knew what those outside the walls and in the villages across England whispered. *Haunted. Cursed.* Rumors he had encouraged over the years when he had been the bandit.

He held the candle up, watching the flame. Anna had asked if they had a chamber she could use where their son could play

so they knew where he was, for the boy liked to hide and send the castle into a flurry trying to find Arthur, who would laugh when his frantic mother held him tight.

The wee lad, already five years old, was always chasing after John's men and jumping out to scare the servants, the small brown dog close on his heels.

As if he had summoned them by thinking about them, Anna stepped into the room, sniffing.

"It smells so much better since we left the shutters open to let the fresh air in the room."

The dog sniffed at the base of the stone wall to John's right, then sat down and barked once, tail wagging.

"Why does he bark at the wall? Is there a spirit?"

Arthur brandished his small sword in the air, the blood-curdling yell ringing through John's head.

"Shall we find out, then?" John ruffled Arthur's hair. He had his mother's green eyes and John's own blond hair. "Are ye not afeared of what ye might find?"

The dog barked again, and Arthur narrowed his eyes. "Nay. I would like to see a hellhound or a dragon." The boy looked hopefully at the wall.

Anna bit her lip. "Do you think it's another passageway? I thought we'd found them all."

John moved closer to where the dog pawed at the stone, moving the candle until the flame flickered. "Mayhap. Look at the flame."

His wife wore her long brown hair braided down her back. She was tiny, almost a foot shorter than he, though she fit him perfectly. With every passing month, she had become more confident. Anna was quiet. 'Twas her nature.

The dog yipped again. Arthur leaned down, stroking the dog's soft fur and whispering into his ear. Both of them had their noses almost touching the stone.

"'Tis not a dragon. A dragon would be too big." He touched the stone. "'Tis cold, so 'tis a spirit. The stable boys say Blackmoor is full of them." He pressed his forehead against the stone as if he could see through the walls. "I do not see any spirits."

John pressed several stones before one shifted then gave way. The sound of stone grinding against stone made him grit his teeth. A cloud of dust filled the chamber, making them cough. When it cleared, the opening was revealed. Arthur chortled, clapping his hands, while the dog barked and ran around his legs.

"Here we go again." Anna sighed, waving a hand in front of her face. "I hope we don't find another skeleton," she mumbled.

The candle held in front of him, flickering wildly, John stepped into the gloom, following the dog, as the animal bounded into the passageway.

There was a stomping noise, and Anna shrieked. "I hate spider webs. I'm always afraid they'll crawl into my ears or nose while I'm sleeping."

"The spiders are more afeared of you than you are of them, wife." John smiled, feeling her take hold of his tunic.

She snorted. "That's what you think."

"No one has been here in a long time." John examined the floor, the dust undisturbed except for the tracks from a dog and a small boy. The dog's barks sounded fainter, as did his son's laughter as they vanished into the darkness.

"Arthur. Don't go too far ahead," Anna called out. "I swear. All those stories you've told him about being the bandit of the wood have him looking for treasure in every nook and cranny of the castle." Her warm breath tickled John's ear.

"What of the stories you tell him at night of monsters, dragons, and giant sharks?"

When his wife didn't like what he said, she simply pretended she hadn't heard him. "Do you know he would not let anyone out of the kitchens until they gave him a piece of cheese? Arthur told them he needed it to catch a giant mouse that would lead him to a mountain of jewels."

Hoping he sounded grave, John said, "Arthur is a boy. 'Tis what boys do. In time, he will find his path in life."

She snorted. "Not as a bloody pirate, he won't."

"Did you swear?" He grinned, his boots loud on the stone.

"I only swear when necessary." She sniffed. "It's cold in here. I'm glad I have my cloak."

"I'll keep you warm, wife." He was going to press her up against the wall and warm her all the way to her toes when they came to a door set into the stone. Cursing, he held the candle up to the wood, looking for a sign or carving to tell him who had built the passageway, but 'twas simply a door, not an answer to the mystery.

The old wood would not give, so John put his shoulder to the door and pushed. There was a creak, a groan, and then door screamed across the stone as it opened into a chamber he had never seen.

Anna peered over his shoulder. "Where are we? I thought we'd been in every room. Are you sure Blackmoor isn't magic? Maybe it changes while we sleep?"

John snorted but wisely did not call down attention from the fates.

"I'm here. What took you so long?" Arthur called out. The dog joyously yipped at having them all together.

There were torches set into the walls. Using the candle to light them, Anna gasped as the torchlight banished the darkness to the corners of the chamber.

"Is this where you've been hiding your treasure?" She wandered around the room, touching tapestries, piles of jewels, and gold spilling out of chests. A great deal of gold. Old coins John had never seen before.

"I vow, 'tis not mine."

In the torchlight, Anna's gray dress turned silver, her hair the color of autumn, a deep, rich brown. His wife looked young as a lass. Times like these, John felt every one of the eight years that separated them in age.

When she had stopped worrying over her sire back in her future time, when she knew he was at peace, she had changed. The worry left her face and a sense of wonder filled her. John saw everyday places and things made new through her eyes. Looking around the chamber at the treasure, he knew he would gladly give it all away if 'twas a choice between her and riches. She was worth more than a hundred such treasures.

John scratched his chin. "Over the years, I have heard tales of pirates hiding treasure at Blackmoor but never believed 'twas true. I thought 'twas a tale told to keep people away."

She whirled around to face him, a hand at her throat. "Do we need to worry about them coming back? There's an absolute fortune here."

"I found a crown. I am King Arthur and Pip is my knight." Arthur indeed wore a gold crown, and enough strands of jewels that John wondered how the boy did not fall over. Pip the dog wore a strand of pearls and rubies as a collar.

Grateful for Arthur making Anna laugh, John picked up a handful of coins. As he suspected, they were old.

"We are inland. Why would such a vast treasure be hidden away at Blackmoor?" he mused aloud as he looked at the mountain in front of them.

"What better place than a haunted castle away from the coast?" she said. "A castle on the coast would be the logical place to look, so it makes sense the pirates or smugglers would go further inland, to the center of the country."

Anna held up an emerald and gold necklace that matched her eyes. "It's beautiful."

John leaned down, ran his hand through an overflowing chest, and picked out the matching bracelet. "An early Yule gift."

"And you didn't even have to buy them." She laughed. "My turn." Anna dug through the goods and held up a ring set with a large ruby. "My gift to you, husband."

"I thank ye, wife." He slid it on his finger—a perfect fit.

Hands on her hips, Anna looked around, nervously

tapping her foot. "Seriously. What do we do with this? Do we try to find the owners? Keep it?"

"The pirates who left their treasure are most likely long dead. 'Tis ours, and I can think of many uses for treasure."

His wife kissed him, tucking a lock of hair behind his ear. "I'm sure you can." She brushed her hands off on her dress. "Come on, we can't stand around staring at gold all day. It's time for supper, and I'm starved."

He left the torches burning. John and a few of his trusted men would return to sort through the fortune and then decide what needs be done. Where it could best be used.

"John?" Anna turned around in the room. "I don't see a door."

Arthur and Pip looked behind a huge tapestry depicting a hunting scene. "It's here, Mother." He hopped up and down, a small dagger in his hand. "This shall be my chamber."

John laughed. "Nay. There is much good to be done with such a fortune." Seeing the sorrow on his son's face, he knelt down to look him in the eye. "You may keep the dagger," he said gently, wrapping Arthur's fingers around the hilt.

"Truly?" Arthur hugged him, sending love through John's heart. Before Anna, he had given up on family. Never thought he would have a home. Believed love was not meant for one such as he. But no man was beyond redemption. And now, now he had all he could ever wish for.

CHAPTER 10

THOMAS AND THE NECKLACE

As Thomas made his way toward the coast, he stopped at an inn called The White Dog because he liked the name. He didn't know why he needed to ride by the sea, but he had quit questioning the feelings that drove him to wander the realm years ago.

He had spent the morn catching chickens that had escaped and were foraging in the woods for what small bugs and bits of green they could find under the thawing snow. In exchange, the innkeeper had fed him and given him a bed for the night.

In the spring, he would visit Josephine and then make his way back to Oakwood. At three score and five years, he could still fight, had not run to fat. Mayhap he would find a battle, lose himself in bloodshed, and forget the dream he had lived with her.

During the winter, the dark came early. Thomas drained the cup of ale, nodded to the servant to bring another, and then sat up straight. Out of the corner of his eye, to the right, was a glint of gold. But 'twas the scent of the warm sun and the call of a raven that had him bending down to check the daggers in his boots so he could get a better look.

Nay, 'twas not possible. It only took three strides before he was across the room and standing in front of three men. This side of the inn was lower, and his head almost touched the roof.

Thomas caressed the hilt of his blade, narrowed his eyes at the ruffians, and snarled, "Where did you get the necklace?"

The man with red hair picked at his teeth with a chicken bone. "We found it. What's it to ye?"

Another pushed back on the bench, hand trembling. "The thing is cursed. Tell him, Rupert."

The one called Rupert belched, showing a mouth full of rotting teeth. "We are minstrels. The necklace was payment."

Penelope would roll her eyes and say if that were true, she'd sell them a bridge. Thomas arched a brow. "Aye? Well then, come on. Give us a tune." He flipped a small coin on the table. The lad who swore the necklace was cursed snatched it as it spun and hid it upon his person.

The men looked to one another. Rupert shifted, his hand going to the blade at his side. Eager for the distraction of a brawl, Thomas bounced on the balls of his feet, a feral grin spreading across his face.

The fight was over before it really began. All three men were sprawled on the floor. Ale dripped off the table and puddled on the stone. Rupert was now missing a few more teeth.

The tale came out, grudgingly at first, then faster, as if they had to unburden themselves of their wrongdoings.

A group of minstrels had played at Ravenskirk Castle, where one of them had stolen the necklace from Lady Ravenskirk. The ruffians had killed the other minstrels after robbing them. One of the men begged for his life and told the ruffians about Oliver. How he had all the silver and goods they had stolen from the houses where they had played, along with a necklace. One of legend, said to be from a fae queen. The man told them where Oliver was going before they killed him anyway. They caught up to him on the road.

"He might be dead; he might live. It matters not." The man spat, and a mouthful of blood hit the stone, mingling with the spilt ale.

"Give it to me or die." Thomas pressed the blade against the man's neck until a red ribbon appeared.

"Hold. I will give it to ye."

He moved the blade enough for the man to dig in the dirty pouch as his waist. With a longing look, he handed over the necklace.

"If you think to lie in wait for me. I will run you through." Disgusted, Thomas re-sheathed his blade. "Be off with ye, before I lose my temper and finish you here and now."

The lad reached in his mouth and pulled a loose tooth free. His eyes rolled back and he swooned, the tooth bouncing across the stone. The others picked up their fellow thief and backed hastily away, the door banging shut behind them.

"Apologies," Thomas said, and dropped a few coins in the innkeeper's outstretched hand. "For the trouble and damages."

The man nodded, grumbling to himself, but Thomas ignored him. He made it to the stables, to an empty stall. Trembling, he found himself sliding down the wall, the cold ground chilling his arse as he stared at the necklace. *Her* necklace.

"How?" Reverently, Thomas touched each charm. The gold chain was heavy in his hands as he held it up, the charms blurring before his sight. No matter. He knew them well.

A sapphire, a diamond, an emerald that reminded him of her eyes, and a gold charm in the shape of a unicorn. Fashioned from the gold in his family ring. He had traded it gladly, knowing Penelope would always carry a piece of him with her. The unicorn 'twas her favorite beast. 'Twas an unusual betrothal gift, but she had not cared for rings, and he thought the charms would be close to her heart, a constant reminder of him.

She had told him every time she gazed upon the sea and the winter sky that the silver color would remind her of his eyes. Thomas blinked, his sight clearing as he saw the broken chain. He would have it repaired. For now, he put the necklace in the bag with his coin. Once the chain had been repaired, he would wear it close to his heart. Perchance it would soothe the restlessness within.

How had Lady Ravenskirk ended up with his beloved's necklace? Had the fates sent Penelope to him?

Filled anew with purpose, Thomas gave the stable boy coin to fetch him food for his journey. He would travel to Ravenskirk, see with his own eyes if she was there, even as his heart told him she was not. And he would hear the tale.

CLARA HAD SPENT the morn in the kitchens with her lady learning how to make gingerbread cookies. They'd laughed as Clara accidently cut off one of the ginger men's heads. Her lady said it was what would become of Albin if he didn't take Clara to wife after all this time. She would swing the blade herself.

"I have found food is the way to a man's heart," Lady Blackford said as she wiped her brow with the apron covering her beautiful green dress. Clara loved the delicate embroidery. The dress had small trees and leaves around the hem, neckline, and cuffs.

"They taste as good as they smell." Clara chewed, holding in a groan of delight. "I have never tasted such."

"And you shouldn't for at least another hundred years or so."

"Lady?" Clara shook her head. She must not have heard her lady correctly.

"Nothing, just talking to myself. Let's stop for today." Lady Blackford washed her hands and dried them on her apron.

"I will hide them as you said." Clara had caught a few of the lads running out of the kitchens with their mouths crammed full of the cookies. She'd chased them with a wooden spoon, threatening to throw them over the walls and into the sea if they stole one more crumb.

"Take one to Albin." Her lady held out the man missing one arm.

Her mouth twitching, Clara thanked her and went in search of Albin.

One of the guards pointed her to the beach. 'Twas a lovely day, and the winter sun warmed her as she walked. As she made her way down the path to the beach, her breath caught. There he was. She wrapped her cloak tight, wound the scarf around her neck, and called out to him.

"I thought ye could not swim." Clara put a hand on her hip, happy to have caught him off guard.

He whirled around. "Clara. You look fetching this day." Albin tugged on the lock of hair that always fell over his eye.

"Thank ye." She held out the offering. "My lady showed me how to make her ginger men. I brought you one. 'Tis still warm from the ovens."

Albin stepped close. His hand brushed hers as he accepted

the cookie. When he opened his mouth to take a bite, he stopped and looked at the cookie, a grin spreading across his face.

"Tell me, Clara. Were ye hungry on the way? Did ye eat his arm?"

"Nay." She pointed at the cookie. "That is a man who did not wed his woman. The fates took his arm for being such a dolt," Clara said sweetly, inhaling the sea air.

"Oh, aye," he said happily, eating half the man in one bite. It took a moment before he stopped chewing and made a strangled sound in the back of his throat, but wisely, he did not say a word.

"Would ye like a bite?"

"Nay, I had one already. An intact man." She looked at the water, watching him from the corner of her eye.

Albin opened his mouth then shut it. He offered her his arm. "Will ye walk with me?" He took another bite of the ginger man.

"Aye, I will." Happy to spend time with him, she licked her lips, tasting the salt.

He walked closest to the edge of the water, sheltering her from the wind.

"Why did ye never learn to swim?" Clara was curious, as she had learned to swim her first summer at Blackford.

"My lady said she would teach me, but when it grew warm, we saw a great beast in the sea. She told me tales of sharks and how they ate sailors, I wouldn't go in the water after that."

He rubbed his arm. "I am not afeared of the beasts, I just wish to die in battle not in the jaws of a great shark."

"Lord Blackford says she makes each tale bloodier and more gruesome every year but that 'tis safe to swim. The beasts prefer other prey." Clara squeezed his arm as they walked.

Albin took her hand in his, the calluses rough against her skin. "Rain will come today. I always know ever since the day I broke my arm."

He looked to the clear sky. "Come. We should turn back before the storm."

Everyone at Blackford knew if Albin said it was going to rain, it would. She let him lead her back to the path.

"Tell me the story again of how you saved our lady." It was how he broke his arm. She'd heard it many times, but in truth, she liked the sound of his voice, so she listened, content to walk back to Blackford, his hand warming her entire body.

CHAPTER 11

MELINDA AND JAMES

JAMES RIVERS, the Red Knight, now Lord Falconburg, had relished battle. Afeard of no man, he sent men to their knees cowering on the field of battle, and yet he stopped abruptly on the threshold to his solar, going cold and sweating at the same time.

"Emma Pittypat Rivers. Your mother is going to cleave my head from my body and mount it on the gates for all to see."

Was it too late to turn and run for the lists? James eyed his daughter and slowly backed away from the disaster.

"You have lived three glorious years. I am vexed you will not see your fourth name day once your mother finds out what you have done." He lifted a black boot, wincing.

His daughter sat on the floor of his solar covered in honey, clapping her fists together and shrieking, "More. More. More."

'Twas in her hair, all over her dress, and covering her bare toes. Where were her shoes?

"Bloody hell." James ran a hand through his hair. He

straightened, shoulders back, the comforting touch of his swords calming him as he plotted.

He stepped to the door, the sound of the honey squishing with every step. There was no one about. Softly whistling, James called to the hounds, who came running, tails wagging.

He knelt down, one knee in a puddle of honey, looking Emma in the eye.

"Do not tell your mother. Ever. This shall be our secret." With a sigh, he sat back on his heels, watching the dogs clean up the sticky mess.

"Don't tell me what?"

"Um…" James cringed at the sound of his wife's voice. He beseeched the fates to send him into the middle of a battle, any battle. But when he opened his eyes, he was staring into narrowed green eyes.

Head held high, James gazed back at her. He was a warrior; he did not cower before anyone, not even his wife.

Her face turned a fetching shade of pink, and James was not ashamed to admit that he dropped his gaze first. Melinda had a fearsome temper and a shrewish tongue when she was vexed. And she was most heartily vexed.

When faced with danger and insurmountable odds, James stood firm. He was not a dolt. He hauled her into his arms, kissing her soundly. She had not run him through yet, so he touched a curl and wound it around his finger.

"Your hair looks like it has been kissed by moonlight."

"All Merriweather women turn gray early." Melinda huffed, but the corner of her mouth turned up.

"You are more beautiful than the first day I met you," he told her, settling her on his lap. "I remember every detail."

"Sure you do. You're trying to save your head." She glared at him.

"You were being chased by ruffians." He fisted a handful

of her hair. "Your hair was glorious. So many colors. Copper, the red of a sunset, and the dark wine color of dried blood."

"Did you compare my hair to blood?" A small smile crept across her face. "You're such a bloody romantic." The blue dress she wore turned her green eyes the color of the forest.

Melinda touched his face, tracing the scar that went from the corner of his nose and down through the outer edge of his mouth to march across his chin and down his neck. Then she did the same to the other scar that ran through his eyebrow and eye, stopping beyond his cheekbone and around his nose. He shivered at her touch, his hands going to her small waist as he crushed her to him, kissing her until she was breathless.

"My warrior queen," he murmured into her ear.

One of the dogs barked as Emma went for the remains of the honey. "More," she said.

"No you don't." Melinda snatched the jar, peering inside. "Emma Pittypat Rivers. You have been very bad to eat all of Mama's honey."

Emma shook her head and reached for the jar. "More, Mama."

"No." Melinda took a step back from her daughter's sticky hands. "Now I can't make Aunt Lucy's ginger candy."

The dogs licked Emma's face, making her chortle. James couldn't hold it in any longer: he threw back his head and laughed.

Melinda tried to look stern but failed. "Oh goodness gracious, what a terrible awful mess you've made." She looked to James. "Might as well let the dogs lick the rest of it off before I bathe her."

Emma shook her head, curls swinging back and forth. "Don't wanna bloody bath."

"Emma Pittypat Rivers. No swearing." Melinda turned to

James. "This is your fault. Taking her to the lists with her wee sword. The other day, she called the cat a whoreson."

He knew better than to laugh, but 'twas hard. His men still jested that Emma swore better than any of them.

James was grateful every day for sending his wife through time to him. He would love her all his days, grateful for every moment with her and his daughter. Every Yule, when the days grew short and dark, he lit a candle, thanking the fates.

"I love you, Melinda." His voice came out in a rasp.

She put her lips to his ear. "Come. Let me bathe Emma and then you can show me how much you love me, my fearsome husband."

James tucked Emma under one arm and ran for the bathing chamber, the sound of his wife's laughter echoing down the corridor.

§

MELINDA STOOD ON THE BATTLEMENTS, the letter clutched in her hand. Her husband had taken pity on the poor messenger traveling between the three castles and had given him an extra bit of coin.

Both of her sisters had tried bribing her. If it had been summer, she would have made Lucy and Charlotte come to her before she told them the juicy gossip. But since it was winter and crappy weather, Melinda took pity on them and told them about Chloe.

How not only did they have a niece, but oh my stars, if only she could see their faces when they found out why cranky Aunt Mildred had been so closed off all those years. Not to mention why Aunt Pittypat walked on the beach a few times a year and came back full of melancholy, her face wet with tears.

Both of Melinda's aunts had loved men who had traveled

from the past to the future. What Melinda wouldn't give for a phone. Or even better, a car, so they could all be together to discuss the details. Wait until they met Chloe. Their niece had grown up knowing Aunt Mildred's man.

"Drat. Why isn't it spring?" She kicked the stone wall.

"Lady? Is aught amiss?" One of the guards took a step closer.

She shook her head. "I am well."

The man turned and went back to watching over the land, alert for any possible sign of trouble. Though, given the weather they'd had this winter, the only trouble Melinda could picture was the Abominable Snowman coming out of the forest and looking to warm himself by the fire.

With the letter from Lucy safely stashed in her pocket so it wouldn't blow away on the wind, Melinda looked out over the land. The small freshwater lakes, called meres, were fed from a spring and stocked with fish.

She remembered the first time she'd laid eyes on Falconburg. With the ponds in front of the castle and the Irish Sea on the other side, it basically turned the castle into an island with only one approach. Talk about intimidating your enemies. Right now, there were chunks of ice floating in the meres, distorting the reflection of the castle.

The oversized scarf Lucy had crocheted was wrapped around Melinda's arm. It was better to be good and cold for her next task. Melinda walked quickly through the house, pausing in the hall to inhale the delicious scents.

The colorful room smelled of dried herbs intermingled with the smell of the fire and warm bread. All she needed now was a big ole mug of hot chocolate. They'd covered replicating pizza, had managed to get hold of citrus and tea, so next on her list was the most difficult item of all. Chocolate. The Aztecs sent it back with the Spanish, so it was a matter of a vessel making the trip, not killing everyone aboard, and, oh right, not screwing up history.

The hall was already decorated for Yule. All of her presents had been hidden away because James was a big snoop. The rugs muffled her footsteps, and the tapestries helped keep the chill away as she made her way through the hall.

She took a breath and opened the door that would take her into the bowels of the castle. Lucy and Edward Thornton had come up with the idea of the ice room. Each of them had set aside a room in the coldest part of the castle. It was basically a rudimentary refrigerator and freezer.

Talk about bloody hard work. Winter ice had to be hauled to the castle and stored in the room, where it was insulated with straw and by the thick walls of the castle. There was a drain to take the slowly melting ice water away.

The expense and effort was well worth it, as the ice kept until early summer. If they filled the ice room, it would likely last more than a year.

Edward had told them his ice kept all year, since he was further north and it didn't get as warm at Somerforth. Last summer, Melinda had surprised everyone after a particularly hard day's work with ice pops.

She'd made them with crushed ice, honey, and fruit juice. They were served in bowls instead of on sticks, but they'd been a huge hit.

The ribbon holding her ponytail had come loose, and as Melinda fixed it, she stopped and stared. There they were, a few more strands of silver. At thirty-five, she was surprised she hadn't turned gray earlier. Lucy's hair was a beautiful silver, so Melinda decided she'd embrace the change. It was too much effort to try to color it. She had other things to figure out. Like chocolate.

CHAPTER 12

CONNOR AND MELLIE

MELISSA EVERS McTAVISH leaned against the doorway to her daughter's bedroom, shocked at the scene before her. Her daughter held Connor's dagger above her head and stabbed the doll, chanting, "Die, evil queen. Die."

"Elana McTavish. What on earth are you doing? And why, may I ask, is Mommy's clay all over the floor?" Her daughter had Connor's dark blue eyes and Mellie's red hair. She was incredibly smart. The way the little gears turned in her head took Mellie's breath away. But right now? Mellie didn't know whether to laugh or run.

Elana sat back on her haunches, the annoyed look on her face so much like Connor's that Mellie almost laughed.

"Dolly is a very bad queen who has turned the realm to eternal winter. If she isn't killed, the world will die. I'm making a clay coffin to bury her deep in the ground. I'll seal the hole with more clay and paint spells on her tomb so no one ever opens it. Otherwise, she'll be really mad we tried to stop her evil plans, and kill us all while we sleep."

It was stated so matter-of-factly that Mellie took a step

back, wondering what on earth was going on with her child, but then understanding dawned.

"Connor," she yelled. "You better get in here right now."

There was a muffled curse, and he appeared in the doorway, dressed in his kilt, weapons plastered across his body, hopping on one foot, a look of agony on his face. He dropped his boots to the floor as he took in the chaos.

"My bonny lass. What did I tell ye about leaving your Hogwarts Lego pieces on the floor?"

Elana smiled her most angelic smile. Just like her father, it usually worked.

"Sorry, Daddy." Then she stabbed the doll again, making Mellie wince. "Mommy is upset I'm casting spells and banishing evil queens."

"Um..." Connor blanched as Mellie narrowed her eyes and tapped a foot. "Is that a new pair of jeans?" He waggled his eyebrows at Mellie, who was having none of it today.

"Did you or did you not let Elana stay up late this weekend and watch the horror movie marathon with you while I was in Charleston for my show?"

The guilty look told her the truth. The two of them loved scary movies that had Mellie covering her eyes.

"Oh, Mommy, it was amazing!" Elana jumped up, twirling around in her pink tutu and leotard, stabbing the air with the dagger as Connor had taught her.

When her daughter was born, Mellie had wondered if Connor would be sad she hadn't given him a son, but he swore Elana was perfect. She wasn't two months old when he made the first dagger for her. It had her name and flowers and vines etched on the blade. There was a dark blue stone in the hilt. Instead of a stuffed animal, Elana slept with the dagger, much to the delight of her husband.

How was it Mellie loved Connor beyond all reason even

as he made her crazy some days? He said she would tire of him if he didn't vex her from time to time.

Elana tugged on Mellie's t-shirt. "We watched *Child's Play, Godzilla, Jaws, Salem's Lot, IT,* and *The Mummy.*" She paused and looked at her father. "What was the one with the wolves?"

Connor slid his blades into his boots. When he saw the look on Mellie's face, he took a step backward, trying to look stern and failing. "That will be enough, Elana. I hope you're happy. Mommy is going to chop my head off."

"Don't be silly, Daddy." Elana rolled her eyes. "Mommy loves you. She's just mad at us." Then their little angel looked up at Mellie. "Don't be mad, Mommy. I love spending time with Daddy." She threw her arms around Mellie, and the scent of strawberries and clay filled her nose as she inhaled her daughter's scent.

"Two of my friends don't have a daddy anymore," Elana whispered to Mellie. The kid was good, Mellie would give her that.

Connor met Mellie's eyes and blew her a kiss before he pulled them both close.

"Daddy, you're squashing me." Elana laughed. "Squish us more. More, Daddy."

"Whatever my little warrior princess wishes." He hugged her until she shrieked with laughter.

It was hard for Mellie to stay mad at him when he smelled so good. His blue eyes promised he would make her forget why she was mad. She leaned closer, his lips a hairsbreadth away from hers.

When he swept her into his arms, to the delight of Elana, and kissed her senseless, Mellie felt boneless. By the time he put her down, she wobbled and the rotten man chuckled, knowing the effect he had on her. Connor ran a finger down the side of her neck. "You and Elana are my heart and soul."

Her husband knelt down, his kilt settling around him as he looked his daughter in the eye. Elana stood with her feet shoulder width apart, her dagger in one hand, the other hand on her hip.

"She is a wee, bloodthirsty lass, is she not? Nay, none of the boys, especially wee Liam from down the street, will be bothering our Elana." He tweaked her ponytail. "What do we think about boys?" Connor demanded.

Their daughter giggled and twirled around. "Boys are awful and they stink." She stopped and patted her father on the cheek. "Except you, Daddy. You smell good."

"Yes, he does," Mellie said, no longer mad.

Connor waited until he was in the hallway before he said, "Ye should thank me, my beautiful wife. Our daughter is fierce and not afraid of monsters."

Mellie picked up a sticky ball of clay and threw it at Connor, who ducked, chuckling.

"She'll have nightmares for months." Mellie sighed.

"No, Mommy. I never have bad dreams. This weekend is the second horror movie marathon. Daddy and I are going to make a fort and have popcorn and ice cream when you go to your show and sell lots of art."

Elana counted off on her fingers. "We're going to watch *Killer Klowns from Outer Space, Cujo, Nightmare on Elm Street*, and… What was the other one, Daddy?"

Connor winked. "*Carrie*," he called out from the safety of the hall. "I have to teach a class. Can't be late."

"We'll talk about your movie choices later," Mellie yelled after him. How could she stay mad when he looked so incredible? What was it about a kilt and a Scottish accent?

With a sigh, she arched a brow at her daughter. "Elana. You are not to speak of these movie weekends to anyone. Not your grandparents, your uncles, or anyone at school.

Some people wouldn't understand you and Daddy's love of scary, totally age-inappropriate movies."

"Yes, Mommy." Elana whacked the doll's head off and was busy encasing it in clay. "Anything else? I have to finish my spells so the bad queen won't escape."

"You have fun." Mellie could just hear the comments if anyone from school or her family heard about her daughter's love of scary movies, daggers, and swords.

Elana was constantly begging Connor for tales of medieval Scotland, the grislier the better. He told Mellie not to worry—when he was a lad, he and his mates were always out and about climbing through old ruins, looking for faeries and monsters.

Connor happily told Elana bedtime stories of battles, of the Thornton brothers, and all sorts of bloody tales. Elana was named after Edward Thornton, who would have never let Connor live it down, but as Connor told the story, the man saved his life, Connor saved Edward's as well, and her husband swore 'twas Edward, not the bloody fates, that sent him to Mellie—so what else could they do but name their first child after the bloody man?

CHAPTER 13

LORD GORGES

LORD GORGES WOKE WITH A START. How much time passed, he could not say. He had not closed the bed curtains before he fell asleep. A sound from the darkest corner of the chamber had him pulling the covers up to his chin.

"It was only a dream." He breathed out, relieved. Until the bells at the abbey rang out, filling him with terror once again.

Soon they would stop ringing and Helena would come to empty the chamber pot, bringing light to the dark chamber. Nay, he remembered he had given her leave to visit her family. The stable boy would not hear him if he shouted, and the cook? Likely drunk and asleep in the kitchens. Peter was utterly alone.

The door to the chamber banged open. Peter shrieked and pulled the covers over his head. The cold that filled the chamber was unlike anything he could remember. The sound of some great thing scraping against the stone made him tremble. Mustering all of his meager courage, he lowered the covers to see a fire blazing in the hearth, filling the chamber with light.

"No," he whispered when he saw the spirit in front of the fire.

The apparition was not his father. This spirit looked like an old man with a white beard, dressed in white robes.

"Who... are... you?" Peter stammered.

"I am the spirit your father foretold. The spirit of Yule past."

The spirit's voice filled the chamber, filling Peter's head until he thought it would split.

Lord Gorges put his feet on the cold stone. Then he pinched his arm. "You are not real, merely an apparition. The stew last night disagreed with me. Sleep. I needs sleep."

But when he blinked, the spirit was still there and holding out a hand.

"Come, Lord Gorges, there is much to see on this night."

Against his will, Peter took the spirit's hand. 'Twas cold to the touch, colder than the snow outside. He flinched and cried out as the spirit took them through the stone wall of his chamber and into London.

On the street, a small boy ran through him, and Peter gasped. "Tell me, spirit, am I dead?"

"Nay, what you see before you is what was." The spirit's voice rang out across the cobblestones. "Look there." The apparition pointed.

It was the house where Peter had spent summers as a child. There was a cousin, a boy named Samuel, who was cruel and threw rocks at him. When he had gone crying to his father, he was told to be a man and fight back. The boy was thrice his size, so Peter spent each summer in terror, never knowing when the next beating or mistreatment would come his way.

'Twas a small comfort to Peter that the boy had died when he had been thrown from a horse and broken his neck.

"Enough, spirit," he cried out, but the spirit took him by the hand, the cold filling his soul, and took him to see *her*.

She had been the daughter of a merchant, well off but not titled or wealthy enough to suit his sire. Peter had loved her with all his heart. His mouth twisted into a snarl as he remembered her telling him that she could never love a man who loved gold more than her. That she loved another, one who would always hold her above all others.

The cottage was little more than a shack. His Iolanthe had married the shoemaker. He pressed his face to the small window and peered through a tear in the parchment. They were seated on stools around a small table, eating soup that looked like little more than water to Peter. And yet, as poor as they were, all of them were laughing, and she looked at her husband and six children with love in her eyes.

"No more, spirit." Peter put a hand to his chest. "I beseech you to take me home. I cannot bear to see such."

The cold from the spirit's hand turned Peter's fingers blue. With one last look over his shoulder, they were no longer in London. When he opened his eyes, Peter was back in his chamber, shivering from the cold. The spirit was gone. With a heavy sigh, Peter climbed into bed and fell into a deep sleep.

LORD GORGES WOKE before the bells at the abbey sounded the hour. He dressed in the dark, ignoring the cold. The fire had gone out, and the hearth was cold as he sat on the stool and waited.

The ringing of the bells sounded loud in the chamber, but the spirit did not appear. Peter waited. And waited until his arse was numb from sitting so long.

"I will not wait. I will find the spirit." He opened the door of his chamber to find himself looking at his chamber. But 'twas different, full of greenery. The chamber smelled of the forest in winter. A fire blazed in the hearth. There was no table—the food was piled on the rug, many types of meats, fruit, and drink.

The spirit sat in a chair before the roaring fire. He was huge, with a torch in his hand, the light turning the chamber to day.

"Come." The spirit beckoned. "I am the spirit of present Yule."

This spirit wore a fine green velvet cloak trimmed with fur and a crown of green upon his head.

"Tell me, spirit. What will you show me so I may profit?"

The spirit drank his wine and stood. "Take hold of my robe."

Peter touched the soft fur. The spirit appeared in front of a small house with holes in the roof and tattered cloth over the windows.

It was the house of his housemaid's family. Peter heard them speak of their sire, now dead. How the man told her 'twas her choice. He would sell her to Peter, or both of her sisters would go in her stead. The girl had sacrificed the love of her betrothed to protect her sisters.

"They are poor yet full of joy," he said.

Helena spoke of the man she loved. She had tried to find him but could not, and did not know if he were still alive.

"Will Helena find her betrothed? Tell me, spirit, will they be together?"

The spirit gazed down at him. "If the future does not change, they will never be together but will die heartbroken and alone."

Drawn to the joy in the small house, Peter peered in the window where the cloth covering had come loose.

"Tell us, Helena. Is Lord Gorges as terrible as everyone says?"

His housemaid nodded. "He is mean, but I pity him. Lord Gorges is alone in life with no one to care for him and with nothing but his gold to keep him company."

Peter stepped back as if struck. The truth of the words sliced him as deeply as any blade.

The spirit turned away from the house. "Take hold of my cloak."

Now Peter found himself in a graveyard. It was cold, and the light of the moon turned the land the pale color of death.

A movement made him stumble. "Spirit. What is beneath your cloak?"

The cloak parted, and the three children dressed in rags who had sought food and shelter stood before him, their eyes haunted.

"They are shivering, spirit. Why do you not feed them?"

"Why should I give of what is mine to feed them? Let them labor for their food and bed. There are too many of those who wish to be given what belongs to others. Let them die for all I care."

Trembling, Peter stumbled over a rock and fell. There before him was a headstone. Cracked and dirty, cared for by no one. The one resting there was unloved and unwanted. Could it be? Was it his?

The abbey bells rang their song, filling the night as Peter found himself abandoned by the spirit.

CHAPTER 14

LUCY AND WILLIAM

"Have you heard from the boys?" Lucy was crocheting a dark blue afghan and took note of her stitch before she looked up.

They were in her solar, each relaxing on a reclining chaise. William had one in his solar as well. He'd been so fond of hers that he hadn't said a word about the cost when she had one made for him for his birthday.

"Aye. There was a skirmish…" He stopped. "I know you do not wish to hear about the fighting when 'tis our sons."

"Tell me… just leave out the gory bits." She took a sip of wine, her hand trembling. Her sons ranged in ages from nineteen to twenty-five. Men. Grown and married with their own babes. But to her, they would always be her little boys.

Peter had twin girls, now five years old and absolute angels. How was it possible she had eight grandchildren?

It seemed like only yesterday she was worried about passing her test for her driver's license. Lucy would never forget the feeling of driving over the bridge to meet her friends for lunch and then to go shopping. It was funny how an hour could last a day yet years passed by in the blink of an eye.

The war would last a hundred years. When she'd been in Holden Beach, there had been international conflicts, but nothing had touched her or her family. Now, though? Lucy had a whole new appreciation for military families and what they went through with loved ones deployed, fighting for their country. What she wouldn't give for a face-to-face call with her sons. Or a text or an email. Normally the slower pace of life never bothered her, but when she was worried about her family, the news couldn't come fast enough.

William told her of the minor skirmishes. The war was in its infancy, so Lucy hoped and prayed somehow history would change. And, if it would not, that her family would be spared. Would grow old and die in their beds after long, happy lives. Shaking her head, she pulled out the last two rows of crochet. She'd repeated the previous row instead of starting the single crochets.

"Have you seen Albin and Clara?" Lucy smiled, thinking of the small boy who, as she had watched him over the years, had grown into a man and the second-in-command of her personal guard.

"Aye. Does he know Clara wishes to wed?" William asked.

Lucy grinned. "He'll figure it out soon enough." She sighed. "Seeing them together… I want all of our family together. Can the boys get leave to come home, just for a se'nnight or fortnight?"

"Perchance if I send a bit of gold and several horses."

"Please, William. I want everyone here in the spring. The children, grandchildren, my sisters, and Chloe." Lucy couldn't wait to meet the newest Merriweather.

"And this man, Richard." William growled. "I will see him in the lists. James heard the man was gravely injured in battle and can no longer fight. 'Tis why the king gave him Bainford Castle. The stones were falling down around the man's head."

She dropped the crochet hook. "What? I can't have my niece living in a hovel. Melinda only said it was obvious Richard loves Chloe, but that they had a few things to work through. What do you know?"

Before she could blow a gasket, William handed her the hook that had rolled across the floor. "After we meet them and ascertain the status of Bainford, we will send men and supplies if needed. After all, she is family."

Lucy wiped a tear from her eye. "She's a Merriweather."

"Do not worry. We will see her properly settled. If Richard is not worthy, I will run him through."

"As much as I'd like that, it might upset Chloe." Lucy tapped her lip. "Christmas is coming. It's the perfect time for a wedding. Clara and Albin are perfect together. Remember when he was a boy? How I horrified him by wearing your tunic and hose?"

William refilled their wine. "Many years ago. Men do not like to be told of how sweet they were as boys. We long to be fearsome."

"You are the most fearsome," Lucy told him, already making plans. "We could invite everyone for the wedding. If the weather clears."

Her husband frowned. "They may be stuck here until spring. Charlotte is with child. Henry may not let her travel." Then, seeing Lucy's look, he said, "He may beg her not to travel." William grumbled under his breath as he paced back and forth in front of the hearth, the rug muffling the sound of his boots.

"I will take stock of the larder. James and those damned Thorntons will eat through our stores in a fortnight."

"Yes, dear," she said absently, concentrating on the pattern of three treble crochet stitches into each space.

&.

THE NEXT DAY, Lucy was in the kitchen cutting out an ornate crust for her apple pie. Once she'd drawn what she wanted, the blacksmith was able to make her a metal cookie cutter. She finished the last leaf and stood back, wiping her brow.

Bertram had been the cook when she'd first arrived at Blackford. He was prickly with her. It was later she'd found out it was because of his injuries that he felt useless.

Once she'd put him in charge of cleaning Blackford, he'd flourished. Lucy blinked away the tears. The man had been in his mid-eighties when he'd passed away in his sleep last year. She still missed his pithy comments. They had a new cook at Blackford, a girl who was scarily efficient.

Charlotte had found her in London and sent the orphan to them. It was grudgingly that Louisa allowed Lucy in her domain. The new cook had been intrigued with the cookie cutters and relented.

"'Tis beautiful, lady." Louisa slid the pies into the oven.

Lucy dusted her hands on her apron. "Thank you. I thought I'd make a batch of ginger candy as well. It's almost Yule."

Louisa tucked a blond lock into her wimple. "Would ye show me?"

"I'd be happy to." Lucy thought for a moment. "Let's see… we need to boil the honey, and then we add ginger, cinnamon, pepper, and saffron."

Louisa looked ill, and the brown dress made her look even more sickly, as it washed out her color. "'Twill be costly."

"William loves the candy, and we'll measure carefully so we don't waste anything."

Times like these, Lucy was grateful she'd found a wealthy lord instead of a peasant. Not that she couldn't love a peasant, but here in medieval England, having money made a huge difference in comfort and not worrying about starvation over a cold winter or during a drought.

"We'll also need breadcrumbs. Once we stir them in, it will make the mixture thick. We'll let it cool slightly, then pour it onto a flat surface and make a rectangle." The kitchen was toasty warm. Lucy imagined her cheeks were as pink as Louisa's.

One of Aunt Pittypat's friends had always said it was just as easy to fall in love with a rich man as it was a poor man. And while Lucy didn't really believe it, deep down she knew she would have adapted if she'd fallen in love with a poor man, though she certainly wouldn't be making ginger candy and crocheting to her heart's content.

"Once the candy has cooled, we'll cut it into squares, put a clove in each square, and post a guard so the wee ones and the men don't steal any." She laughed. "I'll leave you to it. If you have any questions, I'll be outside cooling off."

"My lady?" Louisa bit her lip. "Might you also show me the peepsa?"

"Peepsa?" Lucy blinked. "Oh, pizza." She pulled her cloak around her, blowing cool air down the front of her dress. "I'd be happy to. We'll make it tomorrow."

What harm could it do? A tiny little pizza wouldn't change history. William had fussed at her over the expense until he'd taken a bite. Then he'd been the one to make things happen.

Technically, tomatoes didn't appear in England until the sixteenth century. Lucy remembered Charlotte telling them historians had been unclear on how the fruit had arrived.

They'd snickered in Charlotte's solar because they did know. The abbot from Wintern Abbey, who always visited on his travels, had brought them from Italy after a request and donation from William.

The prior, Father Ashton, raised bees, and the abbey did a thriving business selling mead. Lucy and the prior were responsible for the vast number of beehives dotting the landscape. She'd shown him how to make the ginger candy after he'd expressed a fondness for it.

With their costly greenhouse, and a kitchen maid with not only a green thumb but a green body, Lucy and her sisters now grew tomatoes.

The inhabitants of the castle had developed an obsession with the pizza combinations she'd come up with. Lucy swore they were better than what she'd had back in the States.

Maybe it was the fresh cheese from their own cows and goats, or the crust baked over the wood fire? Either way, she figured since they weren't spreading tomatoes around the country, they wouldn't impact history too much.

Over the years, she'd become proficient at salting and pickling vegetables, using a salt brine from the sea. The vegetables were soaked in water to remove most of the salt when it was time to use them. A family located further down the coast made sea salt that Lucy loved. She traded them honey and her own wool for the salt.

And thanks to the bees, Lucy and her kitchen maids also preserved fruit in honey, so during the winter they could enjoy the fruit.

Even though she'd been in medieval England for over thirty years, some mornings Lucy woke dreaming of Holden Beach, the sun scorching the wooden steps leading down to the blistering sand. She'd run as fast as she could to the water to cool her feet, the tang of salt in the air. Her aunts were so different, and yet, when it came down to it, they looked out for each other.

The garden was barren, asleep for winter. Lucy could have sat in the greenhouse to read, but she wanted to feel the muted sun on her face. The cold air felt good after the stifling heat of the kitchens. The wall protected her from most of the wind as she stretched her legs out. The stone bench was cold beneath her cloak.

There was a skittering on the wall, and when Lucy turned her head, a raven cawed, turning a beady eye on her.

"Hello," she whispered.

The bird ruffled its feathers, seeming to take in the goings-on at Blackford. A chill flowed across her body, like jumping in the ocean in February.

Could it be? "Aunt Pittypat?" Lucy felt silly, but she and her sisters swore the raven had looked out for each of them as they traveled through time. They wished with all their hearts that somehow it was the spirit of Aunt Pittypat in the raven watching over them.

The big bird bobbed its head and, with a caw, flew away, circling once over the castle before going on its way.

CHAPTER 15

ALBIN AND THOMAS

"Clara." Albin held his breath as she stopped on her way to the well. She wore a gray woolen dress with an apron over it. She was so beautiful and kind. He had asked Thomas and the other guards, but the things they told him to say… Albin could not say such to her without sounding like a dolt.

When she smiled, Albin felt like he'd been in the dark and then the sun had come out, turning night to day. He wanted to draw his blade, vow to protect her from all harm, and tell her he loved her.

Did he tell her these things? Nay, he stood there not saying a word, shuffling his feet in the snow like a wee lad.

"Did ye have something to say to me, then?"

Albin could almost see her hair under the wimple. He longed to pluck it away and touch the soft strands. Instead, he thrust a stone at her.

"I found it on the beach. It reminded me of you."

Her hand brushed his as she took the smooth, round white stone, turning it over in her hand.

"I thank ye." Clara looked at the stone then back to him. "How does a stone remind you of me?"

He gulped air. Why had he not asked Lady Blackford what he should say? Why was Thomas not calling for him? The fates were laughing.

"Um... well... 'tis smooth and lovely. Much like you." Albin wanted to jump off the battlements and end this torment.

She looked at him for what felt like a whole day before she smiled. "I will treasure your gift and keep it close." She made sure he saw her put it in the pocket of her dress.

Albin bowed and ran. Nay, he was the second-in-command to his lady—he did not run. He walked swiftly, very swiftly, to the lists, where he did not have to speak of love.

§◦

THOMAS TOUCHED THE NECKLACE, now close to his heart. He'd had the chain repaired before he continued on his journey to Ravenskirk. The weather was clear, and Thomas hoped it would remain so.

Wearing her necklace kept Penelope close to his heart. When they had been together, she would look at him, and Thomas knew she could see into his soul.

The raven was back. The large bird circled once before landing on a tree close to where he made camp for the night. There had been an inn he'd passed, but he would not let his horse stay in what passed for the stables, let alone rest his own head on a bed that moved when he poked it with his blade.

"'Twas a good day. I caught a rabbit," he told the bird. His sister and brother would think him daft, but Thomas felt a kinship with the raven.

Twice it had warned him of danger. Once a band of

bandits, and the second time a trap in the woods he would have fallen in to his death.

If he was asked, not even under threat of death would Thomas admit he believed the bird to be sent from Penelope to watch over and protect him. His family would think he had lost his wits.

The fire warmed him, his eyes heavy as Thomas stretched his feet toward the fire, careful not to singe his boots. They had been a gift from her, and over the years he had kept them repaired, unwilling to let go of something from her.

He caressed the daggers she had given him. One had flowers and vines etched along the steel, with a ruby in the hilt. The second had writing on it and an emerald in the hilt. The writing was French. It said, *You know you're in love when you can't fall asleep because reality is finally better than your dreams.*

As he fell into sleep's embrace, the raven cawed and took flight, startling Thomas. He came to his feet in a crouch and let the blade fly, gratified to hear the scream when the blade found its mark.

The second dagger at the ready, he snarled, "Show yourself or lose your head."

A lad stumbled forward, clutching his shoulder where Thomas' blade was stuck. Face as pale as the snow, the lad stumbled and fell, unmoving.

When Thomas nudged the man with his boot, the lad let out a groan but did not open his eyes.

Shrugging, Thomas braced his foot against the lad and pulled the dagger free. The tang of copper filled the cold night air. The lad cried out, clutching his shoulder, his dirty brown tunic stained and bloodied.

He held up his hands. "I beg ye, do not kill me."

"You think to take me unawares and steal from me, boy?"

The lad wept like a woman.

"Speak, boy."

With a groan, the lad sat up and, through the rips in his tunic and hose, Thomas could see fresh wounds.

"There were bandits… almost killed me. Stole from me," the boy gasped out.

Thomas did not know why he gave the lad a cup of ale instead of running him through. "What is your name?"

"Oliver." The lad's lips were blue.

"Oliver? The minstrel?" Aye, he knew about the lad. 'Twas fate, he supposed.

The lad nodded, shivering as he scooted closer to the fire.

"I am Thomas." He tossed the lad a blanket. "Where is your cloak?"

"They t… too… took it from me." Oliver leaned against the fallen tree, breathing shallowly.

The caw of the raven made the decision for Thomas, though he had to be certain. "Tell me of these men."

As the lad told the tale, stopping often to catch his breath and sip the ale, Thomas frowned. 'Twas the same thieves he had met in the inn.

"They even stole my clothes and cloak. I had to steal what I am wearing." Oliver coughed.

"You stole from the lords and ladies who welcomed you and your fellow minstrels into their homes, paid you in coin to sing, yet you blame the bandits for stealing from you? Tell me why I should not kill you for the thefts?"

"Nay." Oliver cowered. "I must save my betrothed."

The raven cawed once more before taking flight into the deepening night. With a heavy sigh, Thomas rested his elbows on his knees. "There's always a woman, isn't there? Tell me the entire tale."

§

"Albin?" Lucy called to him as he bolted past her.

"My lady?" His face was red, and he was all sweaty.

"What on earth have you been doing? Are we under attack?" He looked like he was about to pass out.

"Nay, lady. I gave Clara a stone I found on the beach. It reminded me of her."

"A stone." Lucy blinked. "What a thoughtful gift. She can carry it with her and always think of you."

His face brightened. "Think ye? I thought I was going to die while I waited to hear if she liked my gift."

Lucy twisted a silver lock of hair around her fingers, thinking. The longer she lived here in medieval England, the more she decided people were the same, had the same desires and wants, no matter the time period.

"You… care… for Clara?" She watched him.

He fidgeted. "Aye, a great deal. But I feel like a dolt when I try to talk to her."

"Does she know how you feel?" Lucy walked through the great hall as they talked, nodding to the servants who were busy finishing the decorations for Yule. She'd been crocheting up a storm and couldn't wait until everyone opened their gifts.

"Nay, I have not told her." Albin looked so despondent that Lucy took pity on him.

"Come. Let us gather holly and place it on Alan's grave."

Every year, she put holly on his grave at Yule and flowers in the summer to mark his passing. He'd been killed when she'd traveled through time. It was Simon's doing, but Lucy felt responsible. So, every year, she remembered him, sat by his grave and told him the news of Blackford so he would know he was not forgotten, no matter how many years passed.

It was all any of us could want, she thought. To be remembered when we were gone. To take comfort in knowing those we left behind cared for us and had not forgotten.

Albin helped her with the holly. When they had enough, he walked ahead, scanning their surroundings for any threat. She knew not to laugh at his seriousness. Not only would it hurt his feelings, but there had been skirmishes and close calls, enough that Lucy knew it was important to always be vigilant. And she'd never forget how Clement had tried to kill her, so no, she would not laugh at her guard doing his duty to protect her.

At Alan's grave, they were silent for a moment before Albin said a prayer and Lucy laid the holly on the headstone.

She pulled her cloak tight around her. The sun was shining, and the sky was clear. She would sit and stay a while. William had a bench placed near the stone when he'd found her there one year talking to Alan as if he had been a close friend.

Touching Albin's arm, she smiled kindly at him, remembering the boy she'd first met so long ago. He'd grown into a fine man, and would make a good husband. He was considerate and caring, yet brutal with a blade when the need arose.

"Albin. You are my favorite of all my guardsmen. Do not tell the others, for it would hurt their feelings."

He finished brushing the dirt off the headstone and saw her to the bench. "Lady?"

"I have watched Clara pine for you. And I see how you watch her." Lucy patted his shoulder. "She loves you. And I'm guessing you love her?"

Albin blinked several times, opening his mouth and shutting it, before he nodded, his eyes huge.

"Good. Then it's all settled. Go. Propose and let us have a Yule wedding."

He gaped at her. "My lady. What if she says nay?"

Lucy rolled her eyes. "Haven't you been listening to a word I said?"

"Aye." He pulled the tunic away from his neck, flapping it back and forth, his face bright red and sweaty.

"Then what are you waiting for? Go. Make the lady yours." Lucy waited a moment and added, "Unless you wish someone else to claim her."

Albin whirled around so fast that she had to turn away so he wouldn't see the grin on her face. She was tired of watching them watch each other. A Yule wedding would be the perfect way to end the year.

"Nay. No one else will have her. Clara is mine." He narrowed his eyes.

"Good. Now go find her and tell her." Lucy took out her crochet project and got comfortable on the stone bench, making sure her cloak was under her so the cold wouldn't seep into her too quickly.

He walked a few steps before turning back. "One of the men is watching over you. He will escort you back to your solar when you are ready, my lady." Albin bowed.

She waved him away. "Leave me alone with Alan. We have much to discuss."

CHAPTER 16

ROBERT AND ELIZABETH

Elizabeth Smith Thornton, now Lady Highworth, stood back, squinting at the painting. It was so cold that she could see her breath. For the past month, she'd been working on a winter scene of the men practicing in the lists. It had been hard to keep it a secret, especially when she'd worked outside, but she wanted to get the movement correct. The painting was going to be perfect in his solar.

Every time Robert found some made-up reason to see what she was doing, Elizabeth quickly threw a sheet over the painting so he wouldn't see what she'd been working on. She tried to work outside, watching the men fight in the lists when she knew he was off doing other things. When he'd ride up, she'd pretend she was painting the courtyard but didn't want him to see it until it was done.

Once he'd figured out she was creating a painting for his Yule gift, he'd taken to popping in and startling her. She'd threatened to make him wear a bell.

"Come inside. You'll catch an ague." His breath warmed her ear and neck as he leaned close.

"You're too slow, husband. I heard you coming." With a

quick kiss on the cheek, Elizabeth gently pushed him back as he made to lift the corner of the sheet. "No peeking."

He pouted. "I am your husband. Can I not see what it is you have been painting? There is no finer swordsman than me, so it must be me. Why would you paint the courtyard when you could paint such a fine specimen such as myself?"

"You are the most handsome of all your brothers," she told him.

"And in all the realm," he added as she laughed. Robert held his hands out so she could admire his tunic and hose. They were a deep burgundy. The tunic was embroidered with gold thread at the neckline, sleeves, and hem with flowers and leaves. He did not care for the current tightfitting fashion. Nor did his brothers. They all complained they could not swing a sword without ripping the garment.

The artist within her wanted to capture his every movement. The sun turned his blond hair to gold and his blue eyes to sapphires. As the fourth son, he'd been content to laze about when she met him. Now? He tended to his estate, took a real interest in everything that happened under his rule, and slowly was coming to see some real issues that plagued the people.

In her old life, Elizabeth Rainbow Smith had been an activist and was arrested numerous times. She'd been horrified by his behavior at first. In time, she'd fallen hard, and now couldn't imagine life without him. Couldn't imagine going back to her time, and didn't want to even if she could.

Elizabeth wrapped her arms around him. "I will tell you what I'm painting."

"Truly?"

Purposely making him wait, she pulled the fur-trimmed hood of her cloak up. "Nope. I'm just teasing. You have to wait until Yule."

At his pout, she laughed and kissed him.

One of the men carried the easel, careful not to smudge the paint, while another packed up her paints and brushes.

"Take it to my solar and put it behind the screen," she told the servant, who nodded. Then she took Robert's arm. "I will lock the door so you cannot go inside."

Robert covered his heart with his hand and staggered backward, earning jests and laughter from the men in the lists. "The lady wounds me."

"Fine." She pursed her lips. "It's a painting of the sky and our home." Robert looked so crestfallen that Elizabeth felt bad for teasing him. "No, love, you're in the painting, but that's all I'm telling you."

He grinned at her. "I knew 'twas so. Now come inside."

"I'll come inside, but you go first, otherwise I know you'll try to peek at your present."

His sigh was dramatic. "If you insist, wife."

As they made their way through the great hall, Robert told her of his day. They spent the afternoons in her favorite room in all of Highworth: the library.

The room was two stories high, with windows over-looking the now-dormant gardens. The smell of the leather and paper made her inhale deeply. It was the best perfume ever.

The warm spiced wine and a platter of bread and cheese was already waiting. The fire crackled in the huge hearth. He took her cloak and saw her settled in front of the fire so she could thaw her toes.

She poured the wine and leaned into him, content as they listened to the sounds of the castle. A few minutes later, Robert chuckled.

"What?" Stiff from standing so long, she rotated her ankles and curled her toes to ease the ache.

"You have red, blue, and green paint in your hair." Robert

pulled her braid loose. "It reminds me of your hair when you first arrived at Highworth."

She scowled at him. "You were such a jerk, or don't you remember?" Elizabeth said sweetly.

"Aye. Even then, I knew you were the only one for me." He pulled her close, the warmth from his body making her drowsy.

"Liar," she mumbled as Tom, the big orange-striped cat, looked up at her with green eyes, then wound around her legs before settling down close enough to the hearth to singe his fur.

He'd been given the title of head rat catcher and had sired a great number of kittens. Robert made sure all families who wanted a cat had one. He told them the fur babies would bring them good luck, though he and Elizabeth both knew it was in preparation for the coming black plague. Both of them hoped the cats would keep the vermin at bay and thereby help keep the plague from touching Highworth or any of their loved ones.

As Robert murmured to her of his plans to celebrate Yule, Elizabeth let the words lull her to sleep.

CHAPTER 17

THOMAS TRAVELS AND DRAKE FINDS
THE PERFECT PRESENT

THOMAS URGED THE HORSES ONWARD. Over the past few days the weather had been mild, and if it held, they would arrive at Ravenskirk before Yule.

"Oliver. What did I tell ye, lad?"

The lad shifted on the horse. "I was looking at the horse. She is beautiful."

Despite his irritation at how slowly they'd traveled due to Oliver's injuries, Thomas had to agree. "Aye, she is lovely."

During their short time together, Thomas had found he missed silence. Even his ever-present companion, the raven, seemed to have had more than enough of Oliver's incessant talking. Penelope would have fled to the beach if she was with them.

When they passed through a village, Thomas had taken Oliver to the healer, and since then, the lad had not looked so poorly nor cried out in his sleep.

Thomas touched his tunic, feeling the charms. How Penelope would have loved seeing his time. Soon he would meet her family, the young girls Penelope had raised as her own after their mother and father had perished. Now they were grown with families of their own. He hoped they would welcome him, understand Thomas had not wanted to leave the only woman he'd ever loved. Or ever would love.

"Might we rest for a bit?" Oliver wriggled in the saddle. "'Tis most uncomfortable."

"Aye, you'll get used to the riding." The minstrel had only traveled by foot, along with his companions. Oliver said he'd only ridden a horse once in his life.

The other minstrels had been stealing from each household, storing the goods in Oliver's belongings. That they had not been caught and punished for the thievery was a surprise to Thomas. The lad might be innocent of those thefts, but he had readily admitted to stealing the necklace, and therefore was a thief. No matter that Thomas could understand what drove Oliver to commit such an act.

Without thought, he pulled the necklace from his tunic, sending a prayer to the fates to watch over Penelope until he joined her in the next life.

Oliver's eyes widened. "Where did you get the necklace? 'Twas stolen from me. I have great need of its powers." He reached for it, almost falling off the horse as Thomas slapped his hand away.

"From the ruffians who took it from you. You have played for a great many lords and ladies. Do you know of the Thornton brothers?"

Oliver blanched. "The necklace belongs to one of them?"

"Aye. To Lady Ravenskirk."

When Oliver jerked, the horse reared, and the dolt slid off the back, landing in the mud. Thomas grabbed the reins in time to keep the mare from running through the forest.

"Easy." A heavy sigh escaped as he dismounted and saw to the animals. "We will camp here tonight. In two days' time, we will reach Ravenskirk Castle."

"I did not know Lord Ravenskirk was a Thornton. I swear it," Oliver wailed.

Thomas met Oliver's gaze. "You will tell Lady Ravenskirk you stole her necklace."

Oliver fell to his knees, the mud covering him from head to toe. "I cannot. The Thorntons show no mercy. They will kill me."

"Mayhap." Thomas shrugged. "Mayhap not. You will tell the lady your tale, and then I will tell my own tale. 'Tis almost Yule—perchance they will take mercy on you. I have heard Lady Ravenskirk is kind as well as beautiful." Thomas looked to the sky, thinking of Penelope. "You will be punished, but she may tell her husband to have mercy, not to run you through after she hears your tale of love."

Oliver's hands shook as he set up the camp. "May the saints preserve me."

Thomas laughed. "I would pray that Lady Ravenskirk is in a mood to forgive. The saints will not save you from her temper."

Not if she had a temper like his Penelope when she was angry. Happy for the first time since returning to his own era, Thomas looked forward to meeting one of the infamous Thornton brothers and, most of all, to meeting Lady Ravenskirk and then traveling on to meet her sisters.

DRAKE HAD BEEN ANXIOUSLY WAITING for the courier to bring the document. Had paid a significant amount to have it delivered on this day.

Millie said she didn't want anything for Christmas, but when he heard from his contact about the auction involving artifacts being sold off from some tiny Eastern European museum, he knew he had to see what medieval items were available.

Ever since Chloe had vanished, they'd searched for her. Drake knew deep in his heart she had done what she'd told them she would as a wee lass so long ago at the cemetery.

She had traveled back in time. But to when? And was she safe? The need to know had driven him to scour everything he could find, but not knowing when to look had made things a bit harder.

Millie had told him to believe Chloe had found her aunts and to look in the fourteenth century when they'd lived, so that was where he'd focused. Thanks to a vast disposable income, he'd found bits and pieces, confirming all three sisters had found each other. But there had been nothing on Chloe. Until now.

Karen would not believe her daughter had traveled through time. Refused to discuss the idea with them. Even Arthur had to admit it was possible. Karen hadn't spoken to her husband for three weeks after that argument. She was convinced Chloe had met an untimely end.

Drake and Millie could not bear to see her so broken-hearted, so he'd hired a firm to aid him in his search. It had been worth every dollar.

It was Christmas Eve, and only one person would be missing at supper tonight. Chloe. Drake's heart clenched for a moment.

Soon. He took a deep breath. Soon he could tell them what he had found out.

Everyone would end the year happy. Karen and Arthur were coming for dinner tonight. Millie had run out to pick up something she'd forgotten on her grocery list before the store closed for the holiday, which left Drake alone to meet the courier.

The bidding had been fierce, with several large museums

involved, but after Drake had seen Lot 31B, he knew he'd bid his entire fortune to have the contents.

Gull Cottage smelled of pine and cinnamon. They had put up a tree in the great room and decorated it with shells and blue and white lights. There were wreaths on the doors, and holiday music played softly through the speakers.

Drake had worried if he was on the porch, he wouldn't hear the knock at the door, so he sat, tapping his fingers on the back of the sofa, looking out at the waves, not even hearing the music playing.

At four score, many of Drake and Millie's friends were content to play bridge and go out to dinner. A few still rode their bikes and walked on the beach. Not him. He taught men how to fight with a blade, and charged them a great deal for the privilege.

There were days he was slower to get up, not as fast with his sword or dagger, but every time Millie entered the room, the years slipped away.

With one smile, he saw the girl he'd fallen in love with. The woman he'd do anything to keep. Drake thanked the fates every night for bringing him to Millie.

And each and every night since she'd left for England, he'd beseeched those same fates to keep Chloe safe. To let her find her destiny and to be happy.

The knock at the door made him jump.

CHAPTER 18

ALBIN WEDS

ALBIN WIPED HIS BROW. He turned from the view of the sea to watch Clara.

She cocked her head. "What are you looking at?" Clara frowned as she smoothed her dress. "Why did ye bring me out here today? The wind is likely to blow me away."

He swallowed a few times, finding the place within himself that allowed him to fight.

"I have always wanted ye," he said softly. When he looked at her, Clara's mouth was open, her arms wrapped around herself.

As she had not run away, he had to believe what Lady Blackford told him.

"I asked Lord Blackford how he knew my lady was the one for him. He said I would know."

Before Albin could continue, a great gust of wind tore Clara's wimple from her. She took a step back, reaching for the cloth, and did not see the rock. Clara tripped and went backward, reaching out for him, toward the cliff.

"No," he called out, his fingers meeting hers, slipping

before he used every bit of strength he possessed to grab hold of her wrist and haul her into his arms.

"Daft woman. You could have been killed," he bellowed.

She blinked up at him as he patted her to reassure himself she was unharmed.

"Clara. You haven't said a word." Albin wrapped his cloak around both of them, their body heat keeping each other warm.

He was so frightened at the thought of almost losing her that the words spilled out of him.

"I have loved ye all my life. When I was but ten, you put a handful of mud down my hose because I laughed at you. I knew then you were the only woman for me."

Clara pushed him back. "Mud? You remember mud?" She glared at him as he rapidly backed away.

"I saved you from certain death," he said. "Do not kill me now."

Her cheeks pink, she narrowed her eyes. "If ye care so much for me, why have ye not done a thing about it? How many years must I wait?" Clara pulled him to her and poked him in the chest.

Something white caught his eye, and Albin picked up the wimple that she had almost died for. It was stuck in a small bit of grass.

"I have tried to catch a glimpse of your hair. 'Tis beautiful. I like it uncovered. The color reminds me of the mud you put down my hose all those years ago."

From her face, Albin knew she could not decide if she should laugh or strike him.

"And you have a fine, wide arse. I watch you as you walk." He could not hold the laughter in. "Do ye know how many of the men I have taken to the lists for looking at your plump arse?"

Clara leaned down, and before he knew what was happening, she'd smashed a handful of mud in his face.

"I do not have a big arse!" She huffed.

It couldn't be helped: he laughed even harder as she threw mud at him until he was covered. He did not try to defend himself.

"Come to me." He reached for her, and she darted out of his reach.

Her skirts flying, she called out over her shoulder, "Catch me if you can."

So he did, running and calling out, hearing her shriek until he could wait no more. He took hold of her and swept her into his arms, her sides heaving as she caught her breath.

"I have loved you as long as I can remember," he told her solemnly.

"Then why wait so long to tell me?" she demanded, her hair smelling of the sea.

Albin ran a finger down her cheek. "I am a dolt."

Then he set her on her feet and dropped to one knee, ignoring the cold and the mud, and held out the ring he'd had made by the blacksmith.

"Will ye be mine? Marry me, Clara."

The ring was simple. A plain silver band. Was it enough? She deserved so much more.

Her eyes filled with tears. "Aye, I will." She held out her hand as he slipped the ring on.

"I dinna think ye would want me. I will never be rich or have my own home, and I will serve Lord and Lady Blackford until I die." Albin couldn't breathe as he waited to hear if she would no longer want him.

Clara took him by the shoulders, though she had to reach up to do it. "Daft man. I have always loved you, wanted you for my husband." She blinked several times. "I do not care if you are rich. Why do we need gold when we have each other? We have a roof over our heads, food to fill our bellies, and a kind lord and lady. What more do we need?"

He had to swallow a few times before he could answer her. "Aye. You are right."

She grinned. "Always remember that and you will make a fine husband." Then she laughed, taking his hand and leading him back to their home.

Along the way, she talked of the wedding, and he was content to be by her side, listening and nodding. Occasionally stealing kisses.

She was his. There was nothing else he needed in life.

LUCY WANTED to inspect the small cottage on the grounds before the happy couple saw it for the first time tonight. She'd had the servants cleaning and decorating for the past two days. There were pretty linens on the bed, a cozy afghan she'd crocheted with wool from her very own flock of sheep, and a bowl with a couple of oranges. A prized gift. All from she and William.

There was also a small jar of honey and one of jam. One of the kitchen girls would bring them bread and cheese to nibble on after the wedding and festivities.

The only thing that would make Christmas even better would have been to have her sisters and Chloe with her. They had managed another letter between them, so she now knew the full tale about Chloe and enough details about Aunt Mildred and Pittypat that she could wait until she saw her sisters and Chloe to find out the rest of the story.

Lucy had finally come the conclusion that she and her sisters were the ones to have come up with the curse. To ensure they all found each other when they traveled back in time. They must have passed down the instructions to their children, and their kids, and so on.

William had promised they would visit Bainford in the spring, or have Chloe and Richard come stay at Blackford.

A wedding on Christmas Eve was the perfect way to end the year.

Back home, Lucy wouldn't have given a second thought to being able to go to a grocery store and buy whatever produce she was in the mood for, no matter the time of year. Now, there were limited choices, and only when fruits and vegetables were in season or came from a coveted jar of jam. Though she was working on freezing both fruits and vegetables by keeping them in the ice room. William had dubiously eyed her science project and suggested they have their enemies try the thawed fruit and vegetables before she killed anyone in the household.

Her greenhouse and her solar were her two favorite places at Blackford, though the icehouse was pretty fabulous.

This time of the year, the oranges were in season. It was amazing the chores children and grown men and women would do for an orange.

After closing the cottage door and smiling at the wreath of holly on the door, Lucy stopped by the house to make sure Clara had everything she needed before continuing on to the chapel.

Between the greenery and beeswax candles, it smelled heavenly inside the chapel. The small stone building was cozy and warm with everyone waiting for the bride to arrive. Albin looked nervous. Lucy saw Thomas catch his eye and point to his feet so Albin would stop fidgeting.

Then the door opened and Clara floated down the aisle in a beautiful blue wool dress to stand next to Albin, her smile as bright as the candles.

During the ceremony, William took Lucy's hand and whispered in her ear, "Were we so besotted with each other?"

Lucy rested her head on his shoulder. "We still are."

"Aye, we are. You'll always be young and beautiful to me, wife." William kissed the top of her head. As Lucy thought back on her time at Blackford, she didn't notice William had put something in her palm. When she opened her hand, she had to clap her other hand over her mouth so she wouldn't disrupt the service.

"I didn't want to wait until the morrow."

He slid the ring on her finger, the gold band softly glowing in the candlelight. The emerald was as big as her thumb.

"It's beautiful. Thank you." She squeezed his hand.

※

AFTER THE FEAST and festivities had died down, William and Lucy brought the couple to the cottage.

"A wife should have a proper home." William clapped Albin on the back, almost sending him to his knees.

"'Tis ours?" Clara's eyes were huge.

"Yes." Lucy hugged them both.

"Thank you, my lady, my lord," Albin and Clara said at the same time.

Lucy smiled as Albin carried Clara across the threshold and into their new home.

Turning to go, Lucy found herself swept up in William's arms. She wiped her eyes. "I love weddings."

Her husband cleared his throat. "I thank the fates every day you fell from the sky and found me, my love."

"Take me home, husband." Lucy wrapped her arms around him. "I love you, William."

CHAPTER 19

LORD GORGES

When the spirit came, Lord Gorges was ready.

The apparition was dressed in a black cloak, still and watchful, sending shivers through Peter.

"Are you the spirit of Yule to come?"

The spirit did not speak.

"Spirit. I am ready. Humbled by the things I have seen."

The spirit pointed but did not speak.

Peter's hands shook. This spirit was more frightening than the others. He trembled before the apparition.

"Are you here to show me what has not yet come to pass?" He swallowed. "Is that why you have come, spirit?"

The spirit did not answer him.

The chamber seemed darker, colder. For the first time since he could remember, Peter was chilled to his bones.

"Spirit. I beg you. Speak to me." Wringing his hands, Peter said, "I have been humbled by the things I have been shown. I will change, spirit." He fell to his knees. "I beseech you, spirit. Speak to me."

But the spirit remained silent. Constant.

Weary, Peter whispered, "Let us go, then, spirit. The dawn

will come too soon. Let us be off to see what you must show me."

The spirit did not speak, but Peter found himself carried away by the apparition.

They came to a grand house, the wealthy men talking about one of them who had died.

"Should we go to the funeral?" one asked.

Another sniffed. "I would go if there will be a feast."

"Nay, 'tis cold. We are warm. Let us not be bothered," said another.

Without a word, the spirit took Peter to the dead man's house. The few servants were stealing from him.

"No one will miss him," the woman spat.

A boy grinned. "He won't miss 'em. Let us take it all. Even the sheets."

"He was cruel," another said.

The spirit carried Peter to the dead man's chamber. There was a sheet thrown over the body. No one had come to prepare it to be buried. The servants ignored the body as they stole even the bed curtains.

Terrified the dead man under the sheet might be him, Peter reached out to the spirit.

"Oh, spirit, I beseech ye. Is there any person who will miss this man? Please, spirit, show them to me."

The spirit carried Lord Gorges to a village square. There a man faced the gallows. He cried out, "I did it for my love. I should not have stolen from the lady. Why did I not wait? I could have taken everything from him after he died. No one would miss him."

Then the spirit carried Peter back to his housemaid. He saw her sisters huddled around her as she wept over her dead lover.

Peter and the spirit watched as Helena waited until her sisters were asleep. Then she walked to the cliffs and jumped to her death.

"Please, spirit," he wailed.

The spirit returned Peter to the cemetery, where he trembled. Peter kept his eyes to the ground. He found he was too afraid to look, to see what might be.

"Tell me, spirit. Is it too late?" Peter wept.

The spirit forced him to raise his eyes, to see 'twas his name upon the cracked and dirty headstone.

Lord Gorges fell to his knees. "Spirit, it is me in that bed. Dead. Unloved and cold."

The spirit's pale hand trembled.

Peter clutched the spirit's cloak, weeping. "Please, spirit. Hear me. I am no longer that man. I will not be that man ever again." He fisted the spirit's cloak in his hands. "Why show me thus if I am truly beyond all hope?"

Peter stared at the hooded spirit, willing the apparition to speak.

"I can change, spirit! I will keep Yule in my heart. And I will live in the past, present, and the future. The spirits of all three shall dwell within me. I shall never forget their lessons. I beg you, spirit, let me wash away this name on the stone."

Peter took hold of the spirit's hand and did not let go, even as the cold made him gasp. And then the spirit changed, diminished until Peter saw he was grasping the bedpost... in his own chamber.

Relief filled him. There was still time for him to make amends.

He called out, "I will live in the past, the present, and the future." Tears streamed down his face. "Oh, Father. I am greatly changed."

Lord Gorges touched everything in his chamber. It was real. Everything had truly happened. He was a changed man.

Laughing, Peter dressed and ran down the stairs. He rushed out of the dark hall to the stables.

"Wake up, lad."

The boy yawned, rubbing his eyes.

"What day is it?"

The boy blinked at him.

"Tell me, what is the day?"

"Yule. It is Yule, my lord." The boy scratched his head, half-asleep.

The scents of the stable filled Peter's nose. "Yule. I have not missed it, then." He was filled with joy. "The spirits did all this in one night. 'Tis a wondrous thing indeed."

Peter reached into the pouch tied around his waist and flipped the boy a coin. "Go, lad. Break your fast and send for a messenger."

The boy bit the coin and grinned.

"Happy Yule," Peter called out as the boy took off.

"To you as well, my lord," the boy said, running as he laughed. The laughter was pure as the freshly fallen snow.

When the messenger arrived, Peter offered him the use of his carriage. He also gave the stable boy another coin.

"Take this letter to Helena. And send a feast. She and her sisters will have a place here. They will no longer be cold, nor will they starve."

While he waited for their return, he sent another messenger to make a donation to the abbey for the care of the orphans he had turned away. A third man was sent to find out about Helena's betrothed.

Lord Gorges had much to tell his housemaid. When Helena and her sisters returned in his carriage, he told her what he knew of her betrothed and the theft.

Helena cried out, "I will lose him forever. He will die for his thievery."

"You will not lose him. He should not have done what he did, but he did it for you." Peter patted her arm. "Do not fret. All will be well."

Full of joy, Peter helped Helena and her sisters light all the candles, torches, and hearths. He sent for greenery and a large feast.

HELENA and her betrothed were reunited. She forgave her love for stealing, and he vowed he would never do it again.

Peter paid the man's debt and saw them married. They lived in his home, had many babes, and were happy all of their days.

From that day on, Lord Gorges became known as a generous and kind man who was loved by his servants. Never again did the spirits visit him. And each and every year, 'tis said his was the most joyous Yule of all.

CHAPTER 20

MILDRED AND DRAKE

"You have been fidgeting all through dinner," Mildred Merriweather scolded her husband. "I even made your favorite, fried chicken." She narrowed her eyes at him, wondering what was going on.

Karen had been a shadow of herself since their darling Chloe had disappeared back in the summer. Even when Millie told her she'd had a dream that Pittypat came to her on the beach, told her Chloe was fine and had found happiness. That Pittypat had sent her husband, Thomas, to find Chloe and to watch out for her for the rest of his days.

But Karen steadfastly refused to believe Chloe had time-traveled, even as she said she accepted Drake had traveled through time and that Mildred's nieces had done the same.

Arthur patted his wife's hand. "I made my famous rum-spiked fruitcake. Who wants a slice?"

"As long as we're not driving," Mellie said, smoothing her silver hair. "That stuff is lethal."

Drake laughed. "I don't want to have to build the police a new headquarters because you crashed into someone's living room on the way home."

"Funny. Very funny." Arthur cut them each a slice of fruit-cake, the smell of rum filling the air.

It was a mild day, in the high fifties, so Millie had opened the sliding glass door to let the salty air in to mingle with the cinnamon and pine.

When they were settled in the great room and had eaten their cake, Drake cleared his throat. Millie had thought he'd left her all those years ago. They'd had a rocky reunion but had come through it stronger than ever. He was so hand-some with his black hair threaded with silver and his blue eyes. Teaching rich executives to fight with swords had kept him young and in good health. It took her a moment to realize he was talking to her.

"Sorry. What did you say?" Mildred took a sip of sweet tea.

"I know we don't open presents until tomorrow morning, but I think we can make an exception for just one."

Drake was so excited that he could hardly sit still. When he grinned at her, she saw the boy she'd fallen hopelessly in love with so many years ago. A warm feeling suffused her entire being. He'd found something.

"I think we can make an exception this one time." Millie leaned forward and reached out for Karen's hand.

When Drake returned from wherever he had hidden his present, he was carrying a flat box wrapped in bright yellow paper with a rainbow-colored bow. Seeing Millie's look, he shook his head, warning her not to say anything.

"Karen. This is for... Well, it's for all of us. But mostly for you." He presented Karen with the gift so reverently that Millie was now sure.

Drake sat down beside her, and she squeezed his hand, wiping a tear from her eye.

"I didn't ask for anything." Karen looked at them with bleak eyes. Her face pale and her hands trembling, she touched the bow. "Bright yellow always makes me think of Chloe, how full of life she was. And the rainbow makes me remember how she loved bright colors." Her voice cracked.

Arthur put his arm around her. "I miss her too. Open the gift." He looked to Millie and Drake, the hope shining on his face as he too grasped the significance of the wrapping.

With a sigh, Karen lifted the lid off the box, the purple tissue paper inside crinkling as she pushed it aside.

Unsure of what she was holding, Millie watched the woman she'd loved as a daughter look at the document encased in a protective sleeve.

"What is it?" Karen looked to each of them and, seeing the joy on their faces, looked back to what she was holding. "The words are too hard to make out."

"Turn it over," Drake said. "I had the translation printed out but wanted you to be able to hold the real thing in your hands first."

She opened her mouth, and a tiny sob escaped, but she waved Arthur away, straightened her spine, and slowly turned over the priceless document

Mellie watched her lips move, saw the tears stream down Karen's face.

"Tell us," Arthur begged her.

But Karen was crying so hard that she shook her head and passed the document back to Drake.

He took the document, turned it over, and read to them. It was almost a diary entry, detailing the sending of goods, servants, and men to a Bainford Castle, where *Lord Bainford and his wife, Chloe Merriweather Gregory, Lady Bainford* resided. The items in question were sent by several prominent families of the time and overseen on the journey by a close friend. Four stood out.

Thomas Merriweather Wilton.

Lord Blackford and his wife, Lucy Merriweather Brandon, Lady Blackford.

Lord Falconburg and his wife, Melinda Merriweather Rivers, Lady Falconburg.

Lord Ravenskirk and his wife, Charlotte Merriweather Thornton, Lady Ravenskirk.

"She really made it." Karen ugly-cried into Arthur's shoulder as he gathered her close.

After a bit, Karen blew her nose. "I don't know how you did it, but I'll never forget this." She sat down between Millie and Drake as the three of them cried together. Chloe had found her nieces. She had married, and… Thomas was there.

❦

LATER, Millie walked on the beach alone, Drake staying behind, knowing she needed a bit of time.

As she walked in the dark, guided by moonlight and the surf, a raven landed on one of the steps leading to a vacation home. It cawed and cocked its head at her.

The tears started again. Millie pulled a tissue from her sleeve and blew her nose.

"I know it's you, Pittypat." She sat down on the step, watching the ancient ebb and flow of the waves.

"Somehow I knew you would make sure Thomas found our Chloe. It was smart for him to use your name, or we wouldn't have known for sure if it was him. I only wish you had met Chloe." Millie paused, looking at the bird, who was solemnly looking back at her.

"Then again, maybe you did." She wiped her eyes. "Thank you, sister." Millie got to her feet and steadied herself for a moment before walking back home. The bird called out three times before flying into the night.

Her nieces, Chloe, and Thomas were together—and, she

thought, happy. Millie had Drake. Karen had Arthur. And Penelope had gladly sent Thomas home, sending her love with him so that, in time, they could watch over Chloe as she too fell through time to find her own knight in shining armor.

For sometimes you had to travel vast distances and fight with everything you had to find your own happily ever after.

CHAPTER 21

THOMAS AND CHLOE ARRIVE AT RAVENSKIRK

CHARLOTTE HAD BEEN busy all day making sure everything was ready for the Christmas Eve feast. Tomorrow was Christmas, or Yule as it was called here, and she couldn't wait.

They had invited all the servants and people from the village for the feast. There was ale and wine to drink. For the meal they had pork, chicken, beef, geese, partridges, eels, almonds, bread, and cheese.

The day after Yule, there would be another feast and apple pie for the immediate household.

Henry opened the door to their chamber, grinning from ear to ear. "Hurry. She's here."

Still thinking about the food, it took Charlotte a moment to switch gears.

"Who's here?" She smoothed her hands down the gorgeous blue dress. It was silk and velvet and embroidered within an inch of its life. Her lady's maid had put her hair up and woven blue ribbons to match the dress through her hair. Though she wore boots under the dress with a dagger in each one.

She wore the amethyst bracelet that had brought her back in time. The one Henry had given her. The amethysts were set in gold. Leaves and flowers carved into the gold. It was exquisite. Henry had given her the matching necklace their first Yule. She touched the necklace, rubbing her fingers across the smooth stones.

"Charlotte. Listen to me." Henry took her hands in his. "Chloe is here." Then he narrowed his eyes. "With the new Lord Bainford. I don't care for the man," he muttered.

"Chloe is here?" She jumped up and down. "Why didn't you tell me?" Charlotte pulled her husband by the arm. "Come on, let's go meet her."

She barely paused to let Henry throw a cloak over her shoulders before they were outside in the courtyard.

"She is still on her horse. My aunts would have my hide."

Henry laughed. "I came to find you first."

"Oh. I appreciate it." She patted his shoulder and looked up at their guests.

"Hi. I'm Chloe, Chloe Merriweather, and this is Richard. Lord Bainford," the girl said.

She was lovely, with long brown corkscrew curls and brown eyes with flecks of gold in them. Her companion looked older. He was muscled and met Charlotte's gaze unflinchingly. All righty, then. She'd leave him to Henry.

"I'm your Aunt Charlotte and this is my husband, Henry." Charlotte pressed her hands to her face. She didn't know where to start. There were so many things she wanted to say. To ask.

So she settled on something easy: "You came in this weather?"

"'Twas the only gift she wanted. To meet her family. How could I refuse?" Richard looked at Chloe, and Charlotte waited a moment before shooting a glance at Henry. By the look on her husband's face, he too had noticed the way

Richard looked at her niece. He'd have to pass Henry's approval, along with William's and James', before he took things further. Poor man. He didn't know what he was in for.

Unaware of her thoughts, Richard continued, "If the weather holds, we will visit Lady Blackford and Lady Falconburg next." He dismounted and offered his hand to Henry. The two men eyed each other, and Charlotte gave them half an hour before they were facing each other over blades in the lists.

Richard lifted Chloe from her horse.

"You're holding my niece a bit close, Bainford," Henry snarled.

"No, uncle. It's fine." Chloe held out her hand, showing off a ring.

Richard looked to them both. "I would ask ye for her hand in marriage."

Henry snorted. "Seems as if you have already done the asking."

"Don't be silly. Richard's only being polite. Getting married or not married is my choice, no one else's." Chloe hugged Charlotte tight. "I can't believe I found you all. I have so much to tell you."

These days, Charlotte cried easily and often. Being pregnant had that effect on her. They fired questions back and forth, laughing and crying when Chloe took a step back, her hand to her mouth.

Henry and Richard unsheathed their blades, looking for what had distressed her, when Charlotte saw their guests.

But it was Chloe who ran to the good-looking older man on the horse. The man barely had time to dismount before Chloe threw herself at him and they all looked at each other, perplexed.

"Granda Thomas," she exclaimed. "I've seen you in so many photographs, heard so many stories." Chloe couldn't stop smiling. "I feel like I know you. You're my Grammy Penelope's husband."

"Aye. That I am." He inclined his head. "Thomas Merri-weather Wilton."

"Shut the front door." Charlotte swayed on her feet and would have collapsed if Henry hadn't held her. "I don't understand. Aunt Pittypat's husband? And you have her name?"

Everyone was talking at once, the sound growing fainter and fainter as Charlotte focused on Thomas. Her hand shaking, she pointed. "Where did you get my necklace?"

Blades were drawn across the courtyard as Henry and his guard surrounded the guests.

Thomas held out his hands. Then he slowly slid a ring off his finger, holding it out to her.

Unable to move, Charlotte was grateful when Henry had one of the men retrieve the ring.

"Look at the initials. And the dates," Thomas said softly. "Penelope had three freckles on her little finger. She taught me to drive her car, and we celebrated my birthday on the same day as your country's birthday. Fireworks are quite the spectacle."

What he said snapped Charlotte back to herself. She clapped her hands together. "Henry?"

Her husband took charge. He had the guard stand down, called for the stable boys to see to the horses, and bellowed for wine.

"Please. Come inside by the fire. We have much to discuss." Charlotte was pleased to note her voice sounded normal, though inside she was a category four hurricane.

FOR ALL SHE KNEW, Charlotte could have eaten cardboard

during the feast. Thomas had shoved his companion forward, and, recognizing the minstrel, Henry had wanted to toss him into the dungeon, until Thomas requested he hear the lad's tale first.

After the meal, and she and Henry had given out gifts, Charlotte couldn't wait another second. Oliver was under guard until Henry decided the lad's fate, but Charlotte was inclined to forgive him. After all, it was almost Christmas, and he'd done it for love.

The four of them sat around the fire in Henry's solar, Chloe and Thomas taking turns telling their tales.

At one point, Chloe turned to Charlotte. "I thought you knew about Granda Thomas?"

"No. My sisters and I knew there was a big secret, but neither Aunt Pittypat nor Aunt Mildred ever told us the truth." Charlotte touched Thomas on the arm. "I am so pleased you made my aunt happy." She wiped her eyes. "I miss her so much."

"Aye, lass. So do I." Thomas looked away for a moment, and when he looked back, his eyes were bright, full of unshed tears. "Meeting you helps." He sat rigid in the chair, as if he were afraid it was all a dream.

Charlotte knew, because she felt the same way. "It does. My sisters will want to meet you too." She sniffled, and Henry took her hand, giving her strength.

Thomas told them about the daggers Penelope had gifted them. Showed them to Henry and Richard, who exclaimed over the craftsmanship.

He had tried to give Charlotte back the necklace, but she told him to keep it, seeing how it brought him comfort, as it had done for her so many times.

When Chloe told them the full story about Mildred, the details Melinda had kept out of the letter in case it should fall into the wrong hands… well, Charlotte didn't think she could take many more surprises.

They talked long into the night until dawn broke on Christmas morning. Charlotte thought she had everything she'd ever wanted, but she was wrong.

Because now she had a niece and an uncle. Thomas said he would stay awhile before going to visit her sisters. Henry would talk with William and James. His nosy brothers would likely get involved too, she thought. They were going to send furnishings, servants, and other assorted things Chloe would need for her life in medieval England.

Charlotte told Henry no sword fighting on Yule. He and Richard could have it out tomorrow. As they were opening presents, Chloe spoke up.

"We should write down the list of gifts and who they're from. I'll never remember."

A chill ran down Charlotte's spine. "We will. Maybe your mom and Aunt Mildred will find it… later. Then they'll know you are safe," she said carefully.

Chloe hugged each of them. "Merry Christmas. Or should I say, happy Yule, Y'all!"

ACKNOWLEDGMENTS

Thanks to my fabulous editor, Arran at Editing720.

ABOUT THE AUTHOR

Cynthia Luhrs writes time travel because she hasn't found a way (yet) to transport herself to medieval England where she's certain a knight in slightly tarnished armor is waiting for her arrival. She traveled a great deal and now resides in the colonies with three tiger cats who like to disrupt her writing by sitting on the keyboard. She is overly fond of shoes, porches, and tea.

Also by Cynthia: There Was a Little Girl, When She Was Bad, and the Shadow Walker Ghost Series.

[f] facebook.com/cynthialuhrsauthor

[t] twitter.com/wickedgreens

[i] instagram.com/cynthialuhrs

ALSO BY CYNTHIA LUHRS

Knights Through Time Romances

The Knight Before Christmas

A Moonlit Knight

Time After Time

Beyond Time

My One and Only Knight

Last Knight

First Knight

Forever Knight

Darkest Knight

Lonely is the Knight

Knight Moves

A Knight to Remember

Thrillers

When She Was Good - coming soon

When She Was Bad

There Was A Little Girl

Paranormal Romances

Embraced by Shadow

Born in Shadow

Reborn in Shadow

Iced in Shadow

Desired by Shadow

Lost in Shadow

Made in the USA
Middletown, DE
17 August 2020

15628565R00073